The Fairy Godmother Academy

BOOK 3

Zally's Book

Jan Bozarth

artwork by Andrea Burden

A YEARLING BOOK

Visit us on the Web! www.randomhouse.com/kids

Educators and librarians, for a variety of teaching tools, visit us at www.randomhouse.com/teachers

Visit FairyGodmotherAcademy.com

Library of Congress Cataloging-in-Publication Data
Bozarth, Jan.
Zally's book / Jan Bozarth. — 1st ed.
p. cm. — (Fairy Godmother Academy ; bk. 3)
Summary: When thirteen-year-old Zally Guevara's grandmother gives her the family's magical cacao seed talisman, Zally dreams her way to Aventurine, an enchanted land where fairy-godmothers-in-training awaken their individual powers.
ISBN 978-0-375-85185-8 (pbk.) — ISBN 978-0-375-95185-5 (lib. bdg.) — ISBN 978-0-375-89335-3 (ebook)
[1. Fairy godmothers—Fiction. 2. Fairies—Fiction. 3. Magic—Fiction. 4. Grandmothers—Fiction. 5. Hispanic Americans—Fiction.] I. Title.
PZ7.B6974Zal 2010
[Fic]—dc22
2009026420

Printed in the United States of America
10 9 8 7 6 5 4 3 2 1
First Edition

Random House Children's Books supports the First Amendment and celebrates the right to read.

Praise for *Kerka's Book*

"This sparkling combination of action and magic is bound to enchant."
—*Kirkus Reviews*

"Excellent. . . . The writing is refreshingly well done and weaves together the author's knowledge of art, folklore, and botany to paint a magical world where readers' senses are piqued by the likes of stone fairies, cave anemones, and a queen named Patchouli."
—*SLJ*

"Great for girls who love fairies and magical worlds."
—KidzWorld.com

Praise for *Birdie's Book*

"Bozarth's tale is a beguiling mix of magic, adventure and eco-awareness, and her message of girl-power and positive change will resonate with tween readers."
—*Kirkus Reviews*

"A fun, light read that ought to be a hit with girls who like adventure and magic."
—Books for Kids (blog)

"Bozarth has taken the best aspects of various young adult genres and mixed them together in a fresh and optimistic way."
—Kidsreads.com

The Fairy Godmother Academy

Birdie's Book

Kerka's Book

Zally's Book

Dedicated to my friend Meredith Dreiss
and my Cuban family

Contents

1

The Bakery

The last Saturday in October, a week after my thirteenth birthday, was awesome. Autumn in New York City can have practically any kind of weather, from warm Indian summer, to clear and crisp, to rainy and miserable. That day the trees along the streets of Manhattan wore their most beautiful fall leaves, and there was a hint of chill in the air. It was a perfect day to sleep in, have a lazy brunch, and then go for a walk in the afternoon. I love to wander around with friends, poking through the things that street vendors have for sale, eating hot pretzels, riding the carousel in Central Park, or watching tourists in the horse-drawn carriages.

Unfortunately, there is no such thing as a lazy Saturday in the Guevara family. That's because my parents own a bakery on the Upper West Side, and everybody in our family works there—from my mother's mother down to José Junior (J.J. for short). We all wake up at four in the morning to get the bakery ready to open at six-thirty for the grabbing-breakfast-on-the-way-to-the-office crowd. Sundays are the only exception. The bakery is always closed on Sundays to get ready for the following week.

I hate mornings. I mean, how many thirteen-year-olds even have a job, much less one that starts at the break of dawn? I don't usually argue, but once, after staying up too late looking at my world atlas the night before—studying maps of all the countries I'll probably never get to see—I made the mistake of telling my parents I was too young to work at Alma de Chocolate, which means "soul of the chocolate." In fact, on the sign outside our bakery, below the name, are the words "We Feed the Soul."

Papá had given me a stern look. "It's the family business, *mi'ja*. We all have to do our part." (*Mi'ja* is short for *mi hija,* which is "my daughter" in Spanish, and that's what my parents usually call me. My brothers and friends just call me Zally, though.)

Mamá gave a small shrug and said, "It is not so bad. In many places, children much younger than you go to work."

Abuelita—my grandmother, who is so short

the top of her head only comes to my shoulder—chuckled and said, "In some countries, you are old enough to be married. At least you do not have children of your own to support." She chuckled again.

I haven't complained since. Now I just drag myself out of bed, no matter how sleepy I am, and get going. Once I get my body up and moving, eventually my brain wakes up, too.

That Saturday seemed like most Saturdays at Alma de Chocolate. It's my job to wait on the customers, so that's what I did. I actually like talking to the people who come in and finding out where they've traveled. I ask about what they did and where they stayed, whether there were any cool ruins, and what kind of animals they saw. I want to know everything!

On the counter, we keep a globe that has Guatemala marked with a teensy Guatemalan flag and a sign that says:

A PORTION OF THE PROFITS FROM
ALMA DE CHOCOLATE
GOES TO SUPPORT THE CHILDREN
OF GUATEMALA.
THANK YOU FOR YOUR PATRONAGE.

Anyway, Saturday mornings are slow, and I was doing homework when a man walked into the shop, wearing a baseball cap, a Windbreaker, and a confused expression—definitely a tourist. He had a map of Manhattan and looked disappointed when he saw me behind the counter.

"Oh, I was hoping someone could help me with directions. Never mind," he said, starting to walk out.

Don't you hate it when somebody thinks that you can't possibly know how to do something just because you're young? "*I* can help you," I said, stopping the man in his tracks.

He didn't look like he believed me, but he turned and came back to the counter. "I'm supposed to meet somebody at the Metropolitan Museum of Art—"

"Simple," I said. I whipped out a blank sheet of paper and sketched a map of the route through Central Park from our shop to the Met.

Have I mentioned that I love maps? Maps have been a hobby of mine for as long as I can remember.

The man raised his eyebrows as I labeled the streets and told him what landmarks to watch for. I loved his look of surprise. He bought a loaf of bread, a mini magdalena, a couple of chocolate *besitos,* and a cup of coffee. Then, thanking me, he left with a smile on his face.

I sat back down, feeling like a true New Yorker.

I was born in New York City, but my parents didn't grow up here; they grew up in a tiny village in Guatemala. After they moved to America, they had to work so hard for every penny that now they never take anything they have for granted. Clothes get passed down or given to a homeless shelter. In the bakery we also find a use for everything. Cans, bottles, paper, and plastic go into recyclers. Day-old breads or pastries get donated to a soup kitchen. On top of that, twice a year my mother travels down to Guatemala with a group of volunteers to build schools. Mamá had been gone for over a week on one of these trips and was due back home on Sunday. When I am fourteen, I'll get to go—my first international trip!

My favorite form of "recycling" in our family is that whenever somebody in our neighborhood finds a stray pet that has no tags, they bring it to us at the shop. Then one of us carries the animal home and cleans it up. We also take in animals whose owners can't care for them any longer for one reason or another.

While there were no customers for a few minutes, Abuelita watched the shop and I took the trash out. When I opened the door to go back in, I heard a pitiful meow in the alley. Looking around, I saw a plump gray cat with white paws come out from behind the trash cans. It ran right to me and started rubbing against my ankles, purring as if I were its only friend in the world. I picked it up and noticed immediately that the cat was not plump from being well fed. She was pregnant.

"*¡Pobrecita!* I bet you could use a soft bed and some good food," I said. I carried the mommy-to-be into the bakery. With a smile, Abuelita made a shooing motion.

I took our newest stray home, fed her, settled her with Papá and J.J., and was back at Alma de Chocolate in twenty minutes. After washing my hands carefully, I started on a new flyer to post in the window.

The bakery closes at five on Saturdays, and my older brothers, Ed (short for Eduardo) and Antonio ("don't call me Tony"), were there to close down. Abuelita wanted to take the leftovers to a family shelter. My best friends, Malia and Cody, were out of town for the weekend, so I went with her. As an extra treat for the kids, I brought along three kittens.

When we arrived at the shelter, the director, Mr.

Duchet, and two of the older kids helped us carry everything inside. It's funny, but the way those kids lit up, you'd have thought it was Christmas. Not just because of the food, either. They loved the *champurradas, conchas,* and chocolate *empanadas,* of course, but they were excited to see Abuelita.

Mr. Duchet, a tall man with wiry black hair, came to stand beside me. "An intriguing woman, your grandmother. It's magical how she fills a room with warmth."

I smiled. "It's like this everywhere she goes. That's one reason I love to come with her."

"What's in there?" The director pointed to my Little Red Riding Hood basket. I lifted the lid and showed him the three sleepy kittens inside.

"It's all right, isn't it?" I asked.

He smiled. "I think you've got a bit of your grandmother's gift in you."

I walked over to Abuelita and handed sleepy kittens to three of the kids to gasps of excitement. After being passed around and petted, the kittens began to explore, climbing onto kids' shoulders, nosing around, and scampering across the floor. The calico kitten pounced on a shoestring and started pulling it. It was no surprise to me that when our visit was over, Mr. Duchet whispered to Abuelita and me, "Is there any chance we can adopt these furry angels?"

Abuelita grinned.

I nodded at the director. "I think my mother will approve."

That evening, Ed and Antonio went out with friends after dinner, and Papá worked on the quarterly taxes for the bakery. J.J., who is eight, was bored, so I offered to play a game of Go Fish with him. I pulled my long hair into a ponytail and changed into a soft pink-and-white striped tee and black leggings. Then I got the playing cards and coaxed the pregnant cat out into the living room to lie beside the coffee table while we played.

Abuelita sat next to us in a rocking chair, reading, as usual. She didn't even look up from her book when J.J. and I pretended to fight about whether he had stolen all the queens from my hand. I shook my finger at him, he poked me, I poked him back, and the argument turned into a tickle fight.

Once J.J. was in bed, I sent e-mails to friends from the family computer in the living room. Then I went to my room to read. Because our family is large—at least larger than most of my friends' families—my room is tiny. But it's mine, all mine. I don't have to share with anyone.

One whole wall is bookshelves from floor to ceiling. We had to get creative to fit furniture into such a small room, so I have a six-foot-high loft bed. In the open area beneath it is my desk. The pedestals that hold my bed up are also bookshelves, one of which is crammed full of atlases and books about cartography, exploration, mapmaking in ancient times, and geography. By the ladder at the end of the bed, a big floor pillow snuggles into the corner of the room, with a light above it.

I was curled up on the pillow, reading *Alanna* by Tamora Pierce, when Abuelita came in carrying two cups of cocoa. I put my book down and moved the desk chair over beside the pillow, and then we both took a mug of the steaming liquid and drank. Abuelita says she based her special recipe for hot cocoa—which she calls *chocolatl*—on an ancient Mayan recipe.

I took a long sip of the spicy cocoa. For some reason, *chocolatl* reminded me of the stories about a fairyland called Aventurine that Abuelita and Mamá have told me since I was a young girl. They only told these fairy tales to me, not to my brothers, and sharing stories and *chocolatl* among the three women of the family had always been a special time.

"Do you know that there is magic in the cacao?" Abuelita asked.

I smiled. After all, I'm a little old for fairy stories now. But I just said, "Mmm, it's delicious."

"Delicious and *magic,*" Abuelita insisted. Even though our whole family speaks Spanish, she likes to practice her English with us grandchildren (and we have to practice Spanish with her). "Our ancestors, the Maya, and their ancestors before them have known the secrets of the cacao for thousands of years."

"Thousands?" I asked, not quite believing her.

She gave an emphatic nod. "Yes. The people who dig up the old things, the—*¿Cuáles son sus nombres?* What are they named?"

"Archaeologists?" I suggested.

Abuelita nodded again. "Yes. Archaeologists. They find the old, very old, pots with just some little of cacao at the bottom. Also, the cacao beans were *muy valioso,* very valuable. The Maya gave them for presents or used them as money. Sometimes it was a gift when the child reaches a certain age."

It sounded like a strange present to me. I had plenty of friends who had had parties to celebrate growing up, like my friend from school Rachael. She'd had a bat mitzvah. I celebrated my First Communion when I was nine, and Alicia, who lives in the apartment upstairs, had a *quinceañera* when she turned fifteen. But I'd never heard of anybody getting cacao beans as a gift for one of those occasions.

"How old did you have to be for that?" I asked curiously.

Abuelita studied me for a moment with her shining dark eyes. "*Que son mayores de edad.* You are old enough."

"Um, thank you?" I replied, a bit confused. As far as I knew, there were no ancient coming-of-age traditions in our family. Maybe she hadn't understood my question.

Just then, Abuelita pulled a small object from a pocket in her apron and held it up. It looked like some kind of fruit, about the size of a papaya, with a yellowish brown rind. "This is the cacao pod," she said. "A small one, yes, but *muy viejo,* very old. It is *especial*—in our family many generations. It is for you now, *nieta.*"

I accepted the pod carefully. "Thanks," I said.

"Your mother and I are already the *hadas madrinas*—fairy godmothers. You will need this to become one as well," Abuelita said.

That stopped me in the middle of a gulp of *chocolatl.* I sputtered and coughed. "Fairy godmothers? Real ones, like in *Cinderella,* you mean?"

Abuelita explained that the magical abilities of fairy godmothers are passed down from mother to daughter, from one generation to the next. Then she said that fairy godmothers aren't just for people, but for all parts of the earth. I didn't really believe it. I mean, it felt weird talking about magic as if it were real! But as my grandmother spoke, I realized that she and Mamá talked about magic all the time. Finally Abuelita said that I, Zally Guevara, am the heir to the Inocentes Lineage. Each girl in a line of fairy godmothers is born with gifts, and through magic, those gifts can be developed into skills that the fairy godmother can use to help the world for the rest of her life.

"You're trying to tell me that I can do *magic*?" I asked.

"To some people it is magic," Abuelita said cautiously. "The women of the Inocentes Lineage have a special gift for helping innocents—children and animals. You will learn more in Aventurine."

I just stared at her. My lips made the word "Oh," but I didn't say anything as things clicked into place—the way people's faces lit up when they saw Abuelita, the way Mamá helped build schools, the way my family attracted animals. And I'd always liked kids and animals, and they seem so comfortable with me. So that was a gift, huh? Okay, maybe I didn't *completely* believe in Aventurine, but I could accept that the women in our family had an amazing talent.

"Where is Aventurine? Can you show me on a map?"

"You will find it, but not with a map. Aventurine has never been mapped," Abuelita said.

"It should be," I said. "With a map, you can never get lost."

Abuelita clucked. "That is like saying if you have a good recipe, you are a good cook. In truth, to use a map properly, you must know where you are. But there is knowledge that comes from the heart. Even for you"—she touched her hand to her chest—"*el corazon es su mapa.* And you must keep the cacao pod," she said. "It is important."

I had more questions, but I wasn't sure I was ready to ask them. Wouldn't that be admitting that it was all real—fairy godmothers and magical lands? It wasn't that I didn't *want* it to be true, but I needed time to think. I stared down at the cacao pod in my hand. "Okay. I'll keep it safe and always keep it near me. Look," I said, getting up and slipping the pod into my favorite bag, a Maya-patterned one that hung from my ladder. Abuelita seemed to like that.

"Good." She walked to the door of my room and then turned. "Drink the rest of your *chocolatl.* It will help you rest well. Tomorrow morning you can sleep a little late, I think."

2

The Arrival

Something woke me up, but it wasn't an alarm clock; it was a tickling on my nose. I scratched my nose without opening my eyes and tried to go back to sleep. The light was bright, and I wondered if I had overslept. Then I remembered Abuelita had said that I could stay in bed a bit longer.

There it was again, the ticklish feeling, as if a spiderweb were brushing against my face. The thought of a spiderweb gave me a chill, because I'm really afraid of spiders. I opened one eye, only to discover that the tickling came from a set of long whiskers.

A black and white rabbit sat by my head.

Curiouser and curiouser, I thought. How had a rabbit gotten up onto my loft bed? I opened my other eye and looked around. I wasn't in my room, or our apartment, or our building, or—as far as I could tell—even New York City.

I sat up and rubbed my eyes. I was at the edge of a broad grassy meadow. My woven bag from Guatemala was beside me. The grass was a bright spring green, sprinkled with wildflowers. Butterflies fluttered over my head, playing tag with each other. Could I be dreaming?

I picked up my bag and looked inside. The cacao pod was still there. Otherwise, the bag was empty. Putting the strap over one shoulder, I got to my feet and brushed bits of grass from my clothes. I noticed I was barefoot and dressed in the same clothes as when I'd read in my room last night. Had I been too tired to put my pajamas on after drinking *chocolatl* with Abuelita? I couldn't remember.

A few shimmering hummingbirds flitted around the wildflowers and darted off. I turned to look behind me. There, a gurgling stream ran through the center of the meadow. Dozens of willow trees draped their branches along the stream. This place, whatever it was, seemed more natural, more real to me than any place I had ever been—and at the same time, less real.

And suddenly there she was. From between a couple of willows, I saw a lady coming toward me. No, not a lady, a fairy—a real fairy! And not the tiny little you-can-hit-it-with-a-flyswatter type of fairy, but a fairy taller than me with iridescent blue wings that opened and closed like a butterfly's. Flowers twined through her dewdrop crown. Her hair flowed to her knees, and she wore a beautiful gown of the palest lilac. The scent of lilacs hung about her as well. A cascade of tiny silver bells on her earrings made a tinkling sound when she moved her head. She stopped a few feet away from me and said, "Welcome, Zally."

That was when I knew it: I was dreaming. Still, I wanted to be polite. So I gave a small curtsy and said, "Thank you . . . Your Majesty?"

She smiled. "You may call me Queen Patchouli. Come with me." She waved a dainty hand toward the trees. "We should get started right away. Do you have any questions?"

Questions? I had lots of questions! I blurted, "Why—I'm just asleep, right?"

She tilted her head and looked at me. "You may be sleeping in your own world, but you are awake here. And this is no ordinary dream. This is Aventurine. You could spend hours or weeks here while you're asleep in your own world. But you'll wake up in your own bed, and only one night will have passed."

My mouth fell open. "Did you say Aventurine? It—it's real?"

She laughed, and I followed her down to the stream. We began to walk along it, the grass tickling my bare feet.

"Are you the queen of all Aventurine?" I asked.

"I am the queen of the Willowood tribe of fairies," Queen Patchouli answered. "There are many more fairy queens throughout the land, each with her own queendom."

"How many fairy godmothers are there?" I asked.

"How many people are in a family?" she asked me in return.

"How much of my family do you mean? Just my parents and brothers and me? Six. With Abuelita, seven."

The fairy queen said, "That is just *your* family. But how many people are in *any* family?"

"That depends," I answered. "Some families are very small. Or should I include cousins and aunts and uncles and grandparents—great-grandparents, even? There are lots of ways to count family members, so there's no easy answer."

She nodded. "That's how many fairy godmothers there are."

I tried a different question. "Do I *know* any other fairy godmothers?"

"You know your mother and grandmother, don't you? You will learn to recognize others."

"How long does it take to become a fairy godmother?" I asked, trying to get a real answer from her.

"How long does it take someone to become a brilliant musician?" Queen Patchouli countered.

"Everyone's different." I frowned. "Some people don't want to become musicians. Some never get really good at it. Others are great right away. Then there are people who have to work hard for years until they get to the same point."

"Exactly," said Queen Patchouli.

Eventually we passed through a grove of trees, then out into a glade. There, more fairies walked or flitted about doing their work—whatever it is that fairies do. At the center of the glade stood a small desk and chair. On the desk was a stunning leather-bound book the size of a dictionary. I wondered if it might be an atlas, and hurried forward to look.

"This is *The Book of Dreams,* Zally," Queen

Patchouli told me. "Before we discuss anything more, I need you to write your dream in it."

"But I usually don't even remember my dreams," I said.

The fairy queen smiled. "Those are not the sorts of dreams that are entered in *The Book of Dreams.* The book is for your hopes and desires. You could just write a hope for today, but far-ranging dreams are more satisfying for the book."

"Okay," I said, wondering if I really had a choice.

The queen motioned for me to sit at the desk.

I put my bag on the table by the book and sat down. "So Mamá and Abuelita wrote in here?"

"Yes," the queen said, "as the other women of the Inocentes line did before them. But not every girl who *could* become a fairy godmother *does* become one. Some girls choose a different path. And some . . ."

"They don't make it?" I asked.

She nodded.

I swallowed hard.

"So, now you will write in *The Book of Dreams.*" Queen Patchouli waved her hand. A snow-white peacock appeared, strutting toward us. The bird fanned out its sparkling tail feathers proudly, nearly blinding me as they caught the sunlight.

"We need one of your feathers, my beautiful friend," Queen Patchouli said.

Turning its back, the peacock shook itself, sending out a shower of light, and released a glittering white feather from its tail. The plume drifted gently to the ground. Murmuring her thanks, the fairy queen picked up the quill and placed it on top of *The Book of Dreams*. Then she lifted the lid off a shell bowl that sat near the book. Inside was a silver liquid.

"Your pen," she said, touching the feather. "Your ink." She pointed to the shell bowl. "Your paper," she said as the pages turned on their own and opened to a blank one.

"Can I read what Mamá and Abuelita wrote?" I asked.

The fairy queen answered, "Perhaps, but you must write *your* dream first."

I took a deep breath and picked up the feather. I dipped the end into the silver ink and wrote the first thing that rose to my mind.

October 25, 2008

I want to travel to different lands, meet new people, see animals I've only heard of. Plus I want to make a map of my travels. Most of all, I want to make a map of Aventurine, because there isn't one. I want to help other girls who need to find their way, by making a map to help them on their travels, too.

—Zally Guevara

I closed my eyes and pictured what I had already seen in Aventurine. Then, dipping the peacock quill back into the ink, I drew a map at the bottom of the page of the meadow, the willow trees, the stream, the forest, and the fairy glade. The ink dried instantly. A moment later, more details surfaced in the margins, and my silver lines were filled with brilliant colors until the page looked like an illuminated book from the Middle Ages.

A breeze blew in and ruffled the pages of the book again. It opened to a dream written in Abuelita's handwriting. . . .

lly Innocents, by ...
care and to share with them
the Magic of Cacao!!

Mayan Chocolatl

30 magic cacao beans, toasted and ground
1 large vanilla bean, split lengthwise
1 Serrano chile pepper, split lengthwise, seeds removed using
1 pinch Salt
2 sticks cinnamon
4 cups light cream
2 tablespoons fine corn meal, toasted
4 tablespoons honey (to taste)

Boil chile pepper with 2 cups of water until ...
... to one cup. Drain pepper from ...
Then ~~...~~ remove ca...

The pages fluttered, and *The Book of Dreams* closed with a thump. I was still in a bit of a daze when a new question occurred to me. "Abuelita said that we're of the Inocentes Lineage of fairy godmothers—women who help innocents. That's not what I wrote about in *The Book of Dreams,* though. What does making maps have to do with helping innocents?"

Queen Patchouli motioned for me to stand; then she led me down a new path. It looked like it was made of crystal shards, but it was soft against my bare feet.

The fairy queen considered my question before answering. "You will be helping fairy-godmothers-in-training who come after you to find their way when they go on their quests. It is a special gift that you have. No one has mapped Aventurine before. But mapping is not the only ability you will develop on your quest. Simply by going, you will learn many skills you need for helping innocents."

"Quest?" I asked. "What do you mean?"

"You will soon find out," said the queen.

"And what exactly *is* an innocent?" I asked. "How can I tell if someone is innocent?"

Queen Patchouli tilted her head. The tiny bells on her earrings tinkled. "The fairy godmothers of the Inocentes Lineage are not asked to judge who is good and who is evil so much as they are expected to help those who are in need—especially those who cannot help themselves. You will learn to recognize innocents, and you will be drawn to those who most need your help."

¡Ay, mira! That seemed like a lot to expect. I mean, I was just barely thirteen, and I thought working in our bakery was too much responsibility sometimes.

"We are here. You must get ready now," the fairy queen said, glancing down at my bare feet. She made a swirling motion with one hand.

A circle of grass sprang up, like water spraying from a fountain. But instead of falling back down as water would, the ring of grass—almost ten feet high—stayed in place, swaying in the faint breeze. From the edge of the grass circle all the way to my feet, a pathway of springy soft moss, dotted with white flowers, grew in just a few seconds.

"Take your bag," Queen Patchouli said. "Everything that you need will be in there."

Picking up my bag from the ground, I felt for the cacao pod family talisman inside. It was still there. Then I walked down the path and used both hands to separate the stalks of grass at the edge of the circle so I could look inside. The circle was hollow. It formed a tiny roofless room, like a changing room in a store—only alive. I stepped in, admiring the wildflowers that carpeted the ground. There was nothing else in the room.

I slipped the bag off my shoulder, and something sprang out of it. I dropped the bag and backed away. The something looked like a leafless tree branch. It hovered at the same height as the grass of the circle. It started to thicken and become more rectangular; then it elongated in several directions. Little flaps of wood unfolded with a clatter, until a wooden wardrobe stood before me.

Yes, I said *wardrobe.* The dark wood at the base was carved with flowers. From the top of the wardrobe, a sun with a carved face smiled down at me. I was still a bit spooked by the jack-in-the-box trick, so I was very careful when I stepped toward it. Who knew? A whole department store might pop out! Then again, the wardrobe might be filled with fur coats and mothballs, and the back might lead to *another* new world. . . .

As it turned out, neither thing happened. I looked around on the ground for my woven bag, hoping my family talisman hadn't been squashed. I didn't see the bag, so I stood to one side and pulled open one of the wardrobe doors. An ordinary mirror was attached to the inside, reflecting my tense body and cautious expression. Relaxing, I opened the second door. Another mirror. In the wardrobe was a long rod with clothes of every kind and color hanging on it. Below that, there were drawers filled with gloves, belts, hats, and dozens of other accessories. A flat area on top of the drawers displayed all sorts of shoes, boots, sandals, and slippers. And *everything* looked my size!

From outside, the fairy queen's voice said, "Take what you need now. This will be your only chance to prepare for your journey."

How was I supposed to know what I needed? I finally decided that I should be practical. I chose a pair of brown leggings, a light-as-air pink cotton shirt that had billowy sleeves, and a cropped brown vest that reminded me of Guatemala, with flowers embroidered all over it. Then I pulled on a pair of purple boots that went up to my knees. They were made out of a material I'd never felt before—something between silk and leather.

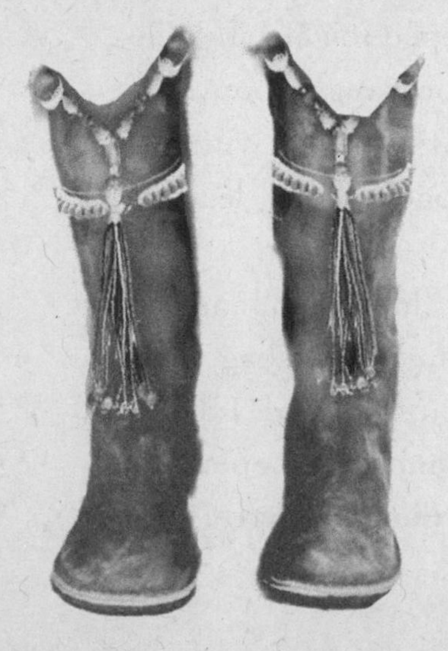

When I was satisfied, I picked up an armful of the clothes I had tried on, to put them back. Suddenly I heard a whooshing sound; then a force like the wind pulled the clothes right out of my hands, except for one long silky scarf, which wrapped itself around one of my wrists. Moments later, all of the clothing—except for what I was wearing and the scarf—had returned to its proper place. Next, even faster than the wardrobe had assembled itself, it shrank back into my bag and disappeared, like smoke being sucked into a vacuum cleaner.

I lifted my bag, half expecting it to weigh a ton, but it felt completely normal. I looked inside. The cacao pod was there. I tucked the scarf, which was the light purple of early dawn, into the bag and slung the bag over my shoulder.

Instantly, the circle of grass around me sank into the ground until it was the same height as all the other grass in the area. I could see Queen Patchouli waiting for me.

"What do you think?" I asked, gesturing to my outfit.

"Perfect. Those are special waterproof boots," the queen said. "I think that you are ready for—"

Just then, a horse and rider galloped up the path and came to a stop right in front of us in a spray of sparkling gravel. The horse, its coat dark with sweat, was a golden palomino with four white stockings and a flaxen mane and tail. The horse shook its head—the mane had golden strands in it, which reflected the sunlight dazzlingly.

Slumped over the horse's bare back was a girl with wild coral-colored hair. Dirt caked her bare legs and was spattered on her arms. Miniature shells dangled from her earlobes and hung from a chain around her neck. She looked about my age and height. Then I noticed her peach-tinted wings, shimmery and sheer like the wings of the other fairies—but one of her wings was broken.

Turning her head toward us, the fairy girl said, "We need your help."

3

The Quest

Queen Patchouli lifted a delicate glass bell, which she rang three times. The sound was not loud and definitely not unpleasant, but the effect was astonishing.

In a flash, fairies appeared from all sides. Some ran, and others fluttered in to land beside us on the crystal path. They each brought something: goblets, strips of cloth, buckets of water, bowls of raw vegetables, long sticks of what seemed to be the slender ends of willow branches, and mysterious bits of violet-colored fluff.

The fairy girl was beginning to slip off the horse's back. Afraid that she might break her other wing, I quickly reached out and caught her. Queen Patchouli helped me lower her gently onto her side on the grass. The girl's dress, woven in a tiger pattern, was torn and muddy.

The horse's sides heaved. An amber-winged fairy set a bucket of water before the horse and let him drink a few sips while an identical fairy covered the horse with a light blanket. The twin fairies then coaxed the palomino to walk in a slow circle to cool down.

The queen swept her arms out wide. The rest of the fairies set to work at an almost feverish pace. A fairy with fuchsia wings offered the fairy girl a goblet filled with clear liquid.

"It should help the pain," Queen Patchouli said.

As the fairy girl accepted the cup, more fairies sat down beside her. They dipped the strips of cloth into the buckets of warm water and wiped dirt from her face and arms. Another fairy untangled her long coral hair with a comb carved from wood.

When the horse was cooled down, the twin fairies removed his blanket. Three fairies with iridescent wings flew in over the horse. They emptied bucket after bucket of cool water over his back, head, and flanks. One of the amber-winged fairies fed him fresh carrots.

During all of the activity, Queen Patchouli very seldom spoke, except to say, "There," or, "Over here, please," or, "Yes, thank you."

Soon, the tiny bits of violet fluff sprang into

action. Although they looked vaguely like purple caterpillars, they moved fast. Dozens of the fluffs hopped onto the horse's coat and jiggled around like miniature scrub brushes, removing dirt from the animal's back. More of the fluffs cleaned the fairy girl, who stayed silent.

When the baths were done, one fairy talked softly to the horse, who kept looking over at the injured fairy with a worried expression. Finally the horse folded his legs beneath him and lay down. He seemed to fall into a deep sleep. Then all the fairies disappeared into the woods. Queen Patchouli picked up several long pieces of whip-thin willow stick and handed them to me. She knelt next to me, beside the injured fairy, who hissed with pain when we had to straighten her broken wing.

"I'm sorry. We'll try not to hurt you," I said.

"Follow this pattern," Queen Patchouli instructed me, tracing her finger along a line in the wing that looked like the vein of a leaf. Even though I wasn't quite sure what I was doing, I watched the fairy queen and tried to do on the front of the wing whatever she was doing on the back, so that my work mirrored hers.

"This is quite a serious break," Queen Patchouli murmured. Her brows drew together with concern. "The Willowood Fairies do not have healing magic for something this serious. All I can do is make a special support for the wing so it can get better on its own." She handed me a soft white strip that looked like a satin ribbon.

"How long will that take?" I asked.

"A year or more," Queen Patchouli answered as she placed a silky strip over the willow splint on her side of the girl's wing and smoothed it down. It stuck in place like the tape they use at a doctor's office.

I did exactly what she had done, and the piece of ribbon on my side of the wing stuck and held the willow in place as well. We both picked up another piece of willow and began to secure the next part of the wing. "A year? Is that normal?" I asked in surprise. "Bones usually heal in a few months in our world. She'll be able to fly before then, won't she?"

The fairy girl's eyes had drifted closed while we worked.

"I'm afraid not," Queen Patchouli said. "If she puts *any* weight on her wing before it is fully healed, she risks a worse break and may never be able to fly again. Only Queen Carmina in the Kib Valley has the healing power that can fully mend this wing."

At this, the golden horse raised his head, shook his mane, and whinnied loudly. The fairy girl's eyes opened wide.

"I am from Queen Carmina's tribe, the Kib Fairies." Tears welled up in her eyes, and she hung her head. "Queen Carmina is . . . unwell," she went on, her voice fainter. "She can no longer heal anyone, including herself."

"Quiet now," said Queen Patchouli. "You and your horse must rest and refresh yourselves. My fairies are preparing food. You may tell us your story while we eat."

We finished splinting the fairy's wing, and Queen Patchouli rang the bell again. Moments later, four fairies came, carrying the ends of a hammock made of willow branches. They lowered it to the ground, slipped it under the fairy girl, then scooped her up in it.

The fairies carrying the injured fairy in the hammock flew away. The queen went to the resting horse and placed a hand on his forelock. His big brown eyes opened and he turned his head from side to side, searching for the fairy girl.

"She is safe," I said soothingly.

"Come this way," the queen said to the horse.

I wasn't surprised when the horse rose to his

feet. After all, this was a dreamland, so why shouldn't a horse understand speech? I wondered if he could speak, as the three of us walked together until the crystal path met another pathway.

We stopped in a clearing where the Willowood Fairies had set up tables in concentric circles. On a raised circle in the center of these tables was another table, this one small and set for three. The fairy girl was already sitting there. Beside the table, a low bench was spread with oats, apples, and alfalfa. Clear water filled a crystal trough. The horse went to the food at once.

Queen Patchouli told me to sit on one side of the injured fairy, and she sat on the other side.

Then the queen rang the bell, and all the fairies sat. Once the whole tribe was seated, Queen Patchouli gently asked the injured fairy to introduce herself and tell her story.

The horse stopped eating and looked up as the fairy began to speak.

"I am Imishi of the Kib Fairies," the fairy girl began. She was still sitting, but her voice carried across the clearing, and she put a hand to the string of shells at her neck. "Some call us the Shell Fairies. And this"—she waved her hand at the horse—"is Kir, prince of the horses of Kib Valley. As most of you know," she said, glancing at me with an odd expression as if she had just now noticed that I had no wings, "our fairy queen, Carmina, is a great healer—or was, until . . ." Her voice broke. She drew a deep breath and started again. "In our valley, we take in animals, fairies, and other creatures when they are injured, sick, or frightened. Our tribe has a gift for healing them, under the direction of Queen Carmina."

I picked up a slice of pink fruit from my crystal plate and ate it while Imishi continued her tale.

"Queen Carmina spoke to me of the Shadeblossom, a rare healing flower that grows only in rocky crevices and at cave entrances. The tiny blooms are a deep indigo color and difficult to see in the shadows. I offered to get some Shadeblossoms for her, but she said it was too dangerous and not worth the risk. Still, I dreamed of finding the flower for the queen, and one day I decided it was too important not to at least *try* to get one."

Imishi looked down and pushed some food around her plate with a slender two-pronged fork. Her cheeks flushed as she continued. "Our valley has high cliffs on one side. I had heard that Shadeblossoms grow outside some of the caves in those cliffs, so I was sure I could fly up to one of the caves, get a Shadeblossom or two, and be back before anyone knew I was gone."

I could feel tension building inside me. When I hear someone telling a story that starts out, "I was told not to do this, but I had a good reason, so I did it anyway," I'm usually pretty sure that things are not going to end well.

"One morning, I awoke early and flew to the cliffs. Once there, I searched for the caves, which are hard to see. I kept seeing something shiny out of the corner of my eye. Finally I saw a cave. I was getting tired and sore, but I flapped as hard as I could and reached the cave opening. Right inside was a single Shadeblossom. I was so excited that I didn't see anything else in the cave. When I did notice a huge shadow coming at me, I stepped backward and fell out of the cave. Almost immediately something caught my fall—something soft, springy, and . . . sticky.

"A *spiderweb*."

I shivered.

"From the ledge above, a giant spider looked down at me. Each of its hairy legs was longer than I am tall."

I stared at the fairy girl. I couldn't even imagine what I might do if I was faced with a spider that big. I could barely deal with a spider the size of a fingernail.

"I tried to get out," Imishi said, "but the more I struggled, the more the spiderweb stuck.

"Just then, Queen Carmina, Azul, Roja, and Blanca—the best fliers from our tribe—showed up. Even though I could tell it saw them, the spider didn't seem to be in any hurry. Maybe it was hoping more of us would get stuck, I don't know. Azul, Roja, and Blanca pulled on my arms and legs, trying to break me free, while Queen Carmina cut through the web with a shell knife. The spider was almost upon us by the time my friends managed to free me. I heard my wing snap as they pulled me away, some of the spider silk still clinging to my wing. The fairies turned to fly away, but the web had caught Queen Carmina's skirt.

"While the queen was cutting herself free, the spider spit its venom at her. It hit Queen Carmina in the face, in her eyes. . . ." Imishi gulped, and tears filled her own eyes. She swallowed hard and then continued. "It happened just as the last strand of web gave way under her knife. Blinded, she flew up against the rock and fell. Blanca caught her and just managed to lower her to the ground while the other two fairies carried me down."

Imishi raised her head and looked around. "It's

my fault. Queen Carmina is scarred and blind and full of fear. She cannot help the creatures who come to Kib Valley. The rest of us clean the sick who arrive in our valley daily, talk to them, feed them, and give them a place to rest. Some of them we can heal with the knowledge we have . . . but others . . . We cannot save all of those who come to us for help. Queen Carmina will not leave her palace rooms and she will not speak with anyone. She barely eats. I am to blame, so I must be the one to find a way to help her. Prince Kir came with me for the sake of the queen and for the sake of his sire, King Xel, who is gravely ill and is not likely to live without Queen Carmina's healing skills."

The horse whinnied—startling everyone for a moment—and nodded his head.

"How long has it been since you left?" Queen Patchouli asked.

The fairy girl looked even more downcast. "Weeks, I think. Prince Kir has never been out of the Kib Valley." She shook her head. "I'm afraid"—her voice was very small now—"I'm afraid we got lost. I actually meant to ask the Kalistonia Fairies for help, but"—she gestured around—"here I am."

Queen Patchouli sighed. "This is grave news. The fairies of Willowood have no particular healing powers. If your own tribe does not know how to aid your queen, I fear we would do no better. But you do need help. Many *innocents* could die if Queen Carmina cannot begin healing the sick again."

The fairy queen gave me a look.

I knew what I had to do. "I'll help," I offered, my voice echoing in the clearing.

Imishi's face fell. "What can *you* do? You're just a child—not even a *fairy*. This is a true emergency. How could you possibly be of help?"

I opened my mouth to answer, and I was surprised that no sound came out.

The fairy queen spoke instead, her tone firm. "You trust *me,* do you not, Imishi? Then believe me when I tell you that Zally Guevara, a fairy-godmother-in-training from the Inocentes Lineage, is your best hope for saving Queen Carmina."

"Are you certain you and your tribe cannot just fly over the land and find Kib Valley?" Imishi asked.

"It is possible, but that could take weeks—just as your own journey did," Queen Patchouli said. "I am surprised that you don't know that most of the fairy queens in Aventurine rarely venture far from their own queendoms. The one exception is when a fairy-godmother-in-training has completed a quest and then either I or another fairy queen has a vision of the path, so that we can be part of sending a girl on her way back to the waking world. This is the biggest reason that Zally should go with you. If she completes her quest, we will be able to find her—and the Kib Valley—very quickly afterward. Zally will help you find the fastest route back to Kib Valley while we gather supplies for the moment when Aventurine has determined Zally's success."

My stomach gave a lurch. "Wait! What do you mean 'find the fastest route'? I don't have a map of Aventurine!"

Queen Patchouli nodded. "There is no map. But, Zally, you are gifted with an intuition for place and space, which is *why* you are good with maps. This is your chance to learn to use that gift. As you travel and learn, you will make a map—a map unlike any you have seen."

"But how?" I mentally kicked myself for sounding so whiny. Imishi didn't trust me to take on this task, and clearly I didn't trust *myself* to do it.

The fairy queen looked from Imishi to Kir and back to me. In a voice that allowed no argument, she said, "You are a member of the Inocentes Lineage, and the Kib Fairies are healers of the innocents in Aventurine. Who could be better suited to help them? If I did not think you were the wisest choice for this mission, I would not allow you to go. You *did* volunteer.

And now your quest is twofold: you will begin to map Aventurine, and you will guide Kir and Imishi back to Kib Valley by the fastest route and do all you can to help the innocents there. On the way, you will also help the innocents you meet. But first, rest; you leave at dawn."

With that, she rang her glass bell, and the fairies began to clear the tables.

4

The Long Road

After a night sleeping on a bed like a silky cloud, I was amazed at how refreshed I felt, even though I awoke at the crack of dawn. I gave a wry smile. I guess no matter *what* world I'm in, sleeping late is not an option. On the other hand, if what Queen Patchouli told me was right, I *was* still asleep in my own bed in my world. How could I sleep and wake up all inside a dream? Sleep within sleep. Very strange.

I didn't know where Imishi and Kir had slept, but they were up and ready to go by the time I pulled on my fairy travel clothes, hung my bag with the cacao pod in it crosswise over one shoulder, and emerged from the curtains that enclosed my canopy bed.

Imishi had changed into a golden-brown dress the color of Prince Kir. The dress was made from overlapping layers of cloth that started at her shoulders, leaving her arms and wings free, and cascaded from the shell belt at her waist to her knees. Loose and comfortable, it seemed like a very practical travel outfit.

Queen Patchouli, along with four of the Willowood Fairies, was there to see us off.

"I know you're worried," I said, trying to reassure Imishi, "but I'll do my best."

She nodded unconvincingly. Her face was pale, and I wondered if her splinted wing was hurting.

"Prince Kir will carry both of you, along with supplies for your trip," the fairy queen said. She turned to me. "Remember that he is a companion and not simply a means of transportation."

Kir snorted, then dipped his head twice in agreement.

"The Shell Fairies consider the horses of Kib Valley cousins," Imishi said. "We would never ride any horse without its permission."

"That is very wise," Queen Patchouli said, patting the golden horse's flank. One of the fairies beside her came forward, carrying full saddlebags. The fairies asked for Kir's permission—and got a nod—before they slung the packs over his back and secured them with a cinch.

"There is plenty of food for you," the fairy queen went on. "There are only two pods of water in your supplies, but the horses of Kib Valley are known for their ability to locate drinking water, and Prince Kir should be able to find what you need." She looked at me. "Zally, I have these for you."

Another fairy handed me a roll of yellow parchment paper and a speckled brown feather that was about eight inches long. I unrolled the parchment but the sheets were blank.

"For your mapmaking," the queen explained. "Keep these things with you in your bag. You have everything you need now."

"Thank you," I said, wishing that the maps had at least some markings on them to start with for me to use as reference points.

With a mysterious smile, Queen Patchouli showed us another roll of parchment pages. They were blank, too. "We will keep these pages here in the Willowood with us. Our pages are connected to yours with magic. Whenever you draw something on your map, Zally, it will appear on our pages as well.

"And now, our other gifts. Prince Kir, you are to have our gift to you; the blanket beneath the saddlebags is of Willowood fairy silk. It will never rub or chafe. It will help those who you have given permission to ride you to stay on your back, so that you need not worry about them falling. It will work in all but the most extreme circumstances. For you, Imishi, weightless shoes to protect your feet for walking and riding while your wing heals. Lastly," the queen said, handing me another piece of parchment no longer or wider than my hand, "I cannot tell you how or when to use this, but you will know when the time is right."

I looked at the paper. It was a recipe in Abuelita's handwriting! *Chocolatl.*

"Imishi, you must sit back on Kir and fold your wings up out of the way so that nothing bumps them. And, Zally, you must find the way for your companions and guide them on the surest path."

I took a deep breath and nodded.

I must have looked uncertain, because Queen Patchouli gave me a look that reminded me of my mother. "Although I have asked you to lead, Zally, remember that you are not alone." Her eyes turned to Imishi as well. "Success for all of you depends on finding each other's strengths and combining them to solve problems."

"I . . . okay," I said, then looked at Imishi and added, "I guess we'd better get started."

"I am ready," Imishi said. Wincing, she overlapped the halves of her wings, then folded them back and upward so that her splinted wing was neatly tucked in. It looked almost as if she had only one half-sized wing at the center of her back. After that, the fairies helped us up onto Kir. I was in front, Imishi behind me.

A faint feeling of direction unexpectedly tugged at my mind. I remembered the few riding lessons I'd taken from my friend Cody's aunt, who owned a stable upstate. I doubted that a horse prince like Kir would respond well even to gentle kicks or nudges. So I simply wound my left hand into the base of his thick golden mane.

"May I tug your mane, just a little, to show you which direction to go?" I asked Kir. He whinnied and bobbed his head. To my surprise, I *felt* a stronger answer from Kir—as if he was not just saying yes, but trying to reassure me that I could guide our small group on this quest. "Turn this way." I pulled his mane gently in the direction of the feeling that tugged at me, noticing with surprise that I sounded far more certain than I felt.

"All speed and safe travels," Queen Patchouli called after us.

She and her Willowood Fairies rose into the air and waved as we headed down the path and through the trees toward the stream. When I looked back, I could still see the fairies hovering up above the Willowood, watching.

We rode all morning long, following my instincts on which direction to go. It was sunny and just warm enough to be comfortable as Kir alternately walked and cantered. I don't know if it was because Aventurine is a magical place or because Kir is a wonderful horse; either way, Imishi and I seemed to be in tune with him and adjusted to his gait automatically. I loved the sound of the hoofbeats and feeling the sun on my face and the breeze in my long hair as we rode.

You may have ridden a horse before, so I won't explain that part to you, or if you haven't ridden one yourself, you have friends who can tell you how wonderful it is. But here's the part no one usually mentions. First of all, after a couple of hours, you begin to wish that you could sit or stand or lean or lounge in any other position. Second, no matter how exciting your ride is, or how beautiful the scenery is, or how nice the weather is, or how pleasant your companions might be, after four to five hours, riding a horse can get tiring. We stopped every few hours to rest, usually when Kir came across a pond or a stream where we could all drink and splash our faces with the cool water.

I'm pretty sure Imishi's wing was giving her trouble, because whenever something bumped it, all of her muscles tightened up. But she didn't complain. Instead, she would make comments like "This is taking a long time," or "I don't know if I can survive a year without flying." The one that got to me—and only after the tenth time she said it—was "Are you *sure* this is the right way?"

The tenth time she said it, I did get, well, *grumpy.*

I know, I should have been more understanding. Imishi was concerned about her queen and her tribe, and she had a painful broken wing. I almost always get along with people, really I do. But I was doing my best, and I was hungry, and my muscles were sore, and every time she said it, it felt like she meant it personally.

"Look," I said through gritted teeth, "I didn't ask to be the leader here. I never said I knew how to get to the Kib Valley, but Queen Patchouli thought I was—am—your best chance. Plus, I'm pretty sure *you* don't know the way, either, or you wouldn't have gotten lost for weeks trying to find help."

"Well, it looks like I'm still lost and still need to find help," Imishi retorted.

I sighed. "Let's have lunch," I suggested. When I started babysitting last summer, my mother told me one of the easiest ways to get children to stop fighting was to offer them food, not as a bribe but because eating is relaxing and brings people together. It couldn't hurt to try with Imishi.

We sat on a couple of boulders beside a stream. Imishi passed around some of the food from the fairy saddlebags: an oat mixture for Kir and bread for Imishi and me. The bread had nutmeg and cinnamon in it. After eating, we did all seem happier, even though we hadn't talked much. I rinsed my hands and face and drank from the stream. Then I sat on the grass beside the boulders and tried to think of what direction we should go in next.

I took the roll of parchment paper out of the bag at my side, along with the brown quill, thinking that even if I didn't know where I was going, I could map out where we had been, and that might give me some inspiration. Unrolling a piece of the paper, I started to write on it with the quill, only to groan when nothing appeared. I wondered if the ink was stuck. I shook the feather and tried again. No luck. I licked the tip of the quill. Nothing. I tried scratching the tip on the bottom of my fairy boot—a trick that sometimes gets ballpoint pens started. Ink still did not appear.

No ink? But Queen Patchouli had said that I had everything I needed. What was I supposed to write with? Blood? Invisible ink, maybe? I growled with frustration.

"So you really don't know where we're going, do you?" Imishi said. Her voice sounded a little bit smug, a little bit accusing, and very worried. Maybe the food hadn't helped so much after all.

"I'll figure it out," I said. "I just don't know how I'm supposed to draw my map without any ink."

"You must have ink," Imishi said. "Queen Patchouli said you had everything you needed in your bag. So if you needed ink, it would be in your bag, wouldn't it?"

I pressed my lips together. I never thought I'd be annoyed by a fairy. "There is no ink," I said, shooting for Queen Patchouli's firm tone.

"Then you don't need any ink," Imishi replied.

"Yes, I *do,*" I said, trying to control my temper.

"Then you have ink," Imishi said.

"How can you say that?" I asked. "I've looked in my bag; there is no ink."

Imishi shrugged, then grimaced with pain. She took a deep breath and insisted, "Queen Patchouli said you had everything you needed."

"I know, I know! But look!" I snapped, pointing to the parchment paper, the quill, and my bag. I snatched up the bag and emptied its contents onto the grass. Only my cacao pod talisman fell out, with a soft thump. "See? This is it. It's all I have. NO INK." I glared at her.

Her aqua eyes avoided mine, and she said, "The fairy queen would not have lied to us."

"¡Ay, mira!" I exclaimed, throwing my hands in the air.

Kir walked over, neighed, and shook his mane as if he were chiding Imishi and me. I wondered if I was just imagining that he was trying to communicate. Either way, I knew I was being grumpy, and it wasn't really fair of me to take my uncertainty out on my traveling companions. I groaned and ran a hand through the tangle of my long hair, trying to decide what to do.

"Maybe Queen Patchouli forgot the ink," I said, trying for a neutral tone.

Imishi shook her head.

Kir nudged the cacao pod with his muzzle.

I picked it up and put it on my lap. "That's not horse food, Kir."

"Prince Kir would no more take something of yours than you would steal something of his," Imishi said.

The palomino gave an emphatic snort.

My face got warm. She was right, of course. I had just spoken to him as if he were a toddler. "I'm sorry, Kir," I mumbled.

Imishi looked with interest at the cacao pod, which I realized she hadn't seen before. "Did you know that is a magical fruit?"

"Yes," I said. "But how did *you* know?"

"Plants are my specialty. I can sense the magic in that one, though we do not have anything like it in Kib Valley." A fleeting frown crossed her face when she mentioned her home. "We should keep traveling while it is still light."

Kir nuzzled her shoulder.

I sighed. "I know our mission is urgent, but I need to make a map. It's not just part of my quest—if I don't find the right direction, we'll waste time."

Kir bent down and nudged my hand, which was still holding the feather quill.

That nudge gave me the strangest idea. I prodded

the cacao pod with my quill. Nothing happened, of course. I gave the cacao pod a whack against the closest boulder and managed to make a little crack in the shell. Feeling a bit guilty for this treatment of a family heirloom, I wondered what Mamá would think if she could see me now.

Imishi did not try to stop me. "I want to stretch my wings for a while. Let me know as soon as you are ready to go," she said. She climbed onto one of the boulders and unfolded her shimmering wings.

I felt less self-conscious without her looking over my shoulder. I whacked the cacao pod again. Soon it was open far enough that I could get my thumbs inside, and I pushed until it cracked wide open.

The inside of the pod surprised me. It was full of pulpy lumps that looked like slimy garlic cloves. I sniffed. Definitely not garlic. The smell was fruity. I pried out a few beans with my fingers and touched my tongue to the squishy pulp, which tasted sweet and refreshing.

I'm not sure what possessed me then. I ate the pulp, leaving a few almond-shaped beans in my hand. I nibbled one and quickly spat the bitter bean out. Using the quill, I poked at one of the dry cacao beans to see what it was like inside.

You know the hollow tube that runs up the

middle of a feather? Well, when the tip of the quill touched the cacao bean, that tube started to fill up with a dark liquid—kind of like the liquid that goes up and up in the center of a thermometer on a hot day, only this liquid was brown. When the feather looked completely full, I pulled the tip of the quill away and gingerly touched it to the map paper. A small dot of deep brown ink appeared.

"No way," I muttered. There hadn't been any juice in that cacao bean, as far as I could tell, and I had never heard of anybody making ink out of cacao beans. It didn't make any sense.

I put the dry beans into my bag, set the cracked cacao pod on the ground next to me, smoothed the paper down, and began to draw. I drew the ponds and meadows and groves of trees we had gone through that morning, and made a general map of the Willowood from as much as I had seen of it. The knots in my stomach began to untie themselves. This was something I *could* do.

I don't know how long it took, but I couldn't help myself; I kept drawing and drawing. I didn't even look at the parchment anymore, but my hand knew what to do. I was so absorbed that I saw nothing of the world around me, until a voice from behind me said, "I see you found your ink."

I turned and blinked several times before Imishi's face came into focus. I nodded.

"What's that?" she asked, pointing to a detailed picture at the center of the paper.

I studied it in surprise. I didn't remember sketching the image. A kind of magic had been flowing through me. I gave a relieved laugh.

"*That* is where we're going next. It's the shortest way to Kib Valley."

5

The Marsh

After studying my map, I rolled it up and put both it and the quill back in my bag. The open cacao pod had resealed itself and now glittered with flecks of gold. I stuffed the pod into the bag, too, relieved to know that Queen Patchouli had been right and that our family talisman was intact.

Imishi and I climbed up on Kir's back again. Using the sun to get my bearings, I guided Kir along the route from my map. We cantered, walked, galloped, and walked again, until we came to a marshy-looking area. The ground was soggy and Kir's feet sank into the mud. Gnarled trees draped with moss and spiky reeds grew at the edges and in the water. Hundreds of small islands, a few feet wide and a few feet high, were visible in the murky water. The path we needed to take was several hundred feet away across the water, but we had no raft or canoe, much less one large enough to carry a horse.

The route that I had mapped out would take us around the marsh along the water's edge, to where we would reach our next path. A mist rose from the surface of the water and a moldy smell hung in the air, giving me a really creepy feeling.

Imishi drew in a sharp breath. "Look!" she said, pointing.

A snake glided silently through the water between the marshy hillock islands.

"So swimming is not an option," I said, trying to joke. No one laughed. I patted Kir's neck. "This way," I said, tugging his mane in the direction of the solid ground along the edge of the marsh.

Once there, he stepped over dead branches and around stagnant pools of water, avoiding the muddier spots. We rode beneath trees with curtains of gray-green moss over their branches. I pushed some moss aside for Kir, letting it go when we were past it. Suddenly Imishi shrieked. I looked over my shoulder to see her trying to tear away at moss that clung to her hair and folded wings. She shrieked again. I did my best to help her get the moss off. Kir stood, waiting patiently.

"It's just moss," I said when it was all off her.

"Well, it didn't happen to you, did it?" she said, her voice trembling. "I bet if you ever got caught in a giant spiderweb, *you'd* think it was a big deal. If I could fly right now, I could get across that water in two minutes."

I struggled to think of something nice to say.

"There," Imishi said, pointing to a less swampy area that stretched almost all the way across the water—an area that looked solid enough and, while muddy, didn't appear to be treacherous.

"I don't think so," I said. "That isn't the route we're supposed to take." I got out the map and showed Imishi the picture of the swamp. I pulled my finger off the map as the image expanded to show us the details as if we were using a magnifying glass. (Now that was a cool effect! I wondered what else the map could do.) "See?" I said. "We're supposed to go around here, and then over there."

"I don't see any roads," she said, sounding unconvinced.

"There aren't any real roads or paths," I admitted. I traced a line on the parchment with my finger.

"I just *sense* the way we're supposed to go, and that's what I draw on the map. This is the route I sensed, so that's the right path to take."

"But that will take too long. We need to hurry." Worry sharpened Imishi's voice. "Anyway, how can you be certain that what you drew is right? How many will die because you insisted on taking your 'right' path?"

Aren't fairies supposed to be small and cute? I thought as I stared silently at the narrow strip of mud that could cut miles off our journey. What if I was wrong? What if the pathway I drew on my map was merely a suggestion for people who had plenty of time to travel? The muddier route seemed to be a straight shot across one end of the swampy lake. It was late afternoon already; if all went well, we could be across before nightfall.

Kir stood still while I deliberated. My instincts told me to take the longer way, but didn't Imishi have instincts, too? After all, *her* queen, *her* people, *her* home were at stake, and she had been more or less right about the ink being in my bag.

How was I supposed to know what was right?

"Great," Imishi said from behind me. "Now we're not going anywhere. Do you plan to just sit here until nightfall?"

I blinked back sudden tears. I had to decide *something*. "All right! We'll do it your way." I knew my mood was showing, but it was the best I could do. "Let's go." I patted Kir, who seemed to be my only supporter at that point. I had been getting better at guiding the golden horse with just a few words or slight pressure from my hand on his mane.

Kir carefully walked us to where the muddy strip began, his hooves making suck-*plop*, suck-*plop* noises as he walked. He took a step or two onto the path, then started backing up, snorting and shaking his mane.

"What's going on?" I asked. The muddy strip looked just as solid as the ground we'd already ridden across, and I couldn't see what had spooked him. Maybe he had seen a shadow or a reflection on the murky water. "Take it nice and slow," I said soothingly.

Kir balked again, then started forward. To our left, across the larger expanse of the swamp lake, mist gathered, thickened, and drifted into our path. Tiny flecks of light danced and flickered in the vapor.

"What are those?" Imishi asked in a hushed voice.

I had hoped *she* would know. "Swamp gas?" I guessed. "I think some people call them fairy lights."

The fairy girl gave a snort. "Fairies that small? That's ridiculous!"

Kir slowed his pace even more. All around us in the swamp, the brownish water and lazy rivulets had a sinister effect, the water so murky we couldn't tell how deep it might be. Silver mosquitoes and large blue-green beetles hummed all around us. Some of them bit, leaving itchy welts; others satisfied themselves with sipping our sweat. Ick.

Kir's withers twitched and his tail flicked. The insects were annoying. Even though the fairy garments that Queen Patchouli had given me were magical and marvelous, right now I would have settled for basic bug repellent.

"I didn't expect so many bugs," Imishi said.

I wondered if that was her way of apologizing. "I hope there's no such thing as a marsh spider," I said. I felt her shudder behind me.

Suddenly Kir slipped into a hidden sinkhole and struggled to regain his footing, spraying mud everywhere. Imishi and I held on tight, despite the magical blanket. Kir plunged toward what looked like more solid ground.

I took several deep breaths, holding tight to Kir's mane and telling myself it wouldn't do any good to panic. Finally he pulled himself onto a rounded hillock covered with slimy weeds. I didn't point out to Imishi that none of this would have happened if we'd stayed on the path I had drawn on my map.

Kir snorted and stomped, shaking his legs to free them of mud. Before we could catch our breath, the hummock beneath us began to tremble and lurch from side to side. Imishi yelped as Kir reared and neighed. The hummock rose, streaming with water, as if it were growing out of the muck. I clung to Kir's mane, and Imishi clung to me. Kir jumped, landing in the mud again but on the opposite side, which I seriously hoped wasn't another sinkhole.

It wasn't.

We landed, spraying more mud and water. We turned and watched as the hummock continued to grow higher and higher with a creepy sucking sound. Then I saw that the hillock was actually a creature—a creature the size of an elephant, covered with weeds and mud. Under its shaggy brown-green coat I couldn't see eyes, only a wide, lipless mouth filled with crooked, squarish teeth.

While my mouth hung open, the creature let out a low moan that was halfway between a growl and a sneeze. Its mouth quivered, and a deep voice rumbled out: "Dooooooo . . . not . . . disturrrrrrrrrrrb." I could see the glowing yellow eyes now behind its drooping nest of muddy reeds. It was my first monster, and I was torn between horror and a weird delight.

My heart hammered in my chest. "Do you know what that is?" I whispered to Imishi.

"It could be a marsh troll, though I have never seen one before," she whispered back.

The marsh troll—or whatever it was—reached for Kir with a massive arm. Kir snorted and tossed his head. Then he danced backward. Imishi screamed in pain as we were jerked back. I thought that she had hit her wing somehow. I shouted for her to hold on. The marsh troll wildly swung a giant hand with three fingers at us. Now *I* screamed and Kir reared.

The troll swung again. Kir sidled sideways to avoid the blow and slid back into the water.

My mind cast about, searching for something, *anything,* that could help us. The marsh troll pounded his fists on the water as if it were doing a drumroll. Pictures started to appear in my mind, distorted pictures with hazy edges: stinging, biting insects; a troll seeking refuge in the water from the insects; a horse landing on the troll's head.

I realized that I was picking up the images from the troll itself! Not really understanding what I was doing, I sent pictures back: calm, murky water; horse and riders leaving him in peace; bugs flying far, far away.

The creature stopped pounding on the water.

I tugged at Kir's mane gently. He slowly turned in the water and walked away from the marsh troll. I sent out more calming visions, wondering what sort of bugs could be so bad that they had angered such a hulking beast.

The troll heaved a noisy, slobbery sigh.

Kir climbed up onto the solid ground. We waited.

The creature sloshed away, and I felt that it no longer meant harm; it just wanted to be alone. It continued to growl as it went, knocking marsh branches and Spanish moss aside, squishing through quicksand pools.

Imishi heaved a sigh of relief, and Kir's trembling stopped.

I realized that the troll was also an innocent. "The troll was just hiding from some giant insects," I said. "It was under the mud so it could have some peace and quiet, and then we stepped right on its head. It just wants to be left alone."

"Well, I am happy to leave it alone," Imishi said emphatically. "Come, we still have a long way to travel before we find the Kib Valley."

Kir stamped his hoof, as if he agreed.

I still felt uneasy and wondered whether to say something. I was pretty sure we were now headed the wrong way, but I knew it was too late to turn back. "Okay," I said. Then I knew I had to at least warn them. "But it still doesn't feel right to me."

"Piffle," said Imishi. "You just don't like that it's not your way."

"No," I responded. "It's not that. But it doesn't matter. You and Kir want to keep going, so let's go. Just don't blame me if this swamp is filled with marsh spiders or something like that."

Soon we came across a portion of the path that seemed to be made up of three marshy islands before the regular mud road resumed. I got a queasy sensation in my stomach, and a faint feeling of dread. The questionable part of the path couldn't have been more than twenty feet long. "Kir, can you stop for a moment?" I asked. "I'm going to get down."

Kir stopped right away. Flinging one booted foot carefully over his neck, I slid off his back. I landed in the mud with my beautiful new boots making a disgusting squelchy sound. "I'll go first," I said to Kir. "I'm lighter than you are, and I'll find the solid spots. Then you follow me."

"I don't think I need to get off," Imishi said,

sounding nervous. "I don't weigh very much."

I knew Kir would be able to maneuver better across the muck without any riders. I wondered if she was trying to avoid getting her new shoes muddy—mud being something fairies don't have to deal with as they fly over the landscape—but it was more likely that she was worried that there really were marsh spiders. *Why* had I said that?

I shrugged. "Suit yourself." I took a cautious step onto the first small marsh island. My feet sank into the mud up to my ankles, but otherwise the little hillock seemed stable enough. I was happy that the boots were waterproof. One more step, then another, and I was across the island, ready to go on to the second. With a bit more confidence now, I stepped out onto the next island. My foot slid right out from underneath me, and I fell forward to land face-first—*splat*—in the grassy, wet muck.

If I hadn't been worried for our safety, it might have been funny. But little alarm bells were going off in my head, telling me that this was dangerous, especially for Kir, who was much heavier than I. That was why, when I heard Imishi giggling behind me, I carefully got to my hands and knees and turned to glare at her.

"This was *your* idea," I said. "You should be the one down here in the mud."

Her face turned sober, and she looked away. A wave of fear and skittishness hit me as Kir whickered and rolled his eyes. That was when I made the connection: I was actually feeling Kir's fear! It was *his* nervousness I had felt so strongly before setting off along this road. I was picking up feelings and images, not words. Just as I had sensed what was bothering the troll.

I sent Kir calming thoughts like *It's okay, we're right here,* while I said aloud, "We'll do this together." We had to—there was no turning back now.

Kir stepped forward and put all four hooves on the first island. Still on my hands and knees, I went onward, feeling with my hands for the most solid spot. *There.* "This is solid, but still pretty slippery, and the muck is deeper than on the first island," I said.

Where Kir stood, with mud well past the tops of his hooves, reeds and grass grew in the water alongside the islands. I had an idea. Tearing up handfuls of grass, I spread them flat across the mud. "I think this will keep your hooves from sinking in so far," I explained. I spread another layer on top of that. Kir stepped forward and barely sank an inch into the ooze.

"It worked!" Imishi said, sounding surprised. "Just one more."

I got back to my feet, steadied myself, and faced the next island. The mud road was just a few feet beyond it. I stepped onto the top of the small hillock. This island felt more solid than the first, and I quickly brought my other foot over. I stamped on the mound to show my companions how solid it was. "See? This one's easy."

But when Kir started to follow me, all chaos broke loose.

Clouds of glowing insects swarmed out of the little island beneath me. In moments, the air was so thick with them I could hardly see. A couple flew into my mouth, and I coughed and spat them out. I pressed my lips together.

In sheer panic, Kir reared up. I jumped back to avoid his hooves—and plunged into the shallow water between the island and the muddy route we were traveling. Kir leapt onto the third island, reared once more, and jumped over me onto the solid mud. I heard a loud *sploosh* in the murky water beside me.

Wiping muddy water from my eyes, I looked in the direction from which the splash had come. I gasped when I saw only a pair of peach butterfly wings sticking up out of the water. Not even the fairy-silk blanket had been able to keep Imishi on a wildly rearing horse.

"Imishi!" I yelled, choking on a mouthful of gnats. A moment later, she pushed her head above the water, coughing and sputtering, only to breathe in a bunch of the glowing gnats. Her coral hair was plastered to her head, and tiny bugs swirled around it.

Even though my lips were pressed together, one of the swamp gnats flew up my nose. I sneezed, coughed, and tried to blow it out, all the while flailing my arms against the cloud of gnats that had begun stinging. Holding on to my sopping-wet shoulder bag with one hand, I struggled to get the other hand into my pocket to pull out the fairy-silk scarf. When I got it out, I tied it around my nose and mouth to keep more gnats from flying in. Following my lead, Imishi tore a strip off her dress and tied it so that it covered the lower half of her face.

Rivers of panic poured from Kir, who reared and neighed on the muddy route. He could have run away to escape the gnats, but he didn't. With much sliding and falling, Imishi and I scrambled up the slope toward the muddy path.

"Your wings!" I shouted to Imishi.

"Are fine!" she yelled back, but I could see the pain on her face.

When we reached the muddy path by Kir, the fairy girl's weightless shoes barely left an imprint. A flat yellow worm clung to her calf and she shook it off. I was glad to have fairy boots protecting my feet and legs. Who knew what else lurked in the slime Imishi and I had just climbed out of?

Kir stopped rearing. His flanks twitched and he shook his mane, but he stood still while Imishi and I climbed onto his back. It was clear that he wanted us to hurry.

The moment we were seated, Kir took off. I leaned forward, twining my fingers in his mane, and closed my eyes to avoid getting mud and gnats in them. Imishi held on to me tightly. It seemed to take forever—or maybe it was only minutes—before we left the insect cloud behind. Finally Kir stepped onto the solid land on the other side of the swampy lake.

The horse stopped and looked back at me, waiting for my direction. I untied the fairy scarf and took the map out of my bag. Although the bag was wet and muddy, my map was still dry. *More fairy magic,* I thought as I studied the map and looked around us for landmarks.

"There! That wasn't so bad, was it?" I could tell Imishi was trying for a light tone, but her voice shook. "I bet we saved lots of time."

"I don't know." I rubbed my forehead with one hand, massaging it to try to ease the headache that had just blossomed, not even caring that my hand was covered with mud. "I have no idea where we are anymore."

6

The Jungle

Another thing people usually don't tell you about traveling by horse: if you're not used to it, you get sore. I mean *sore*. I mean really, really sore. You learn that there are muscles in your body that you've never used before. So there I was in the middle of Aventurine, tired, headachy, hungry, filthy, and sore in a million different places, with one companion who couldn't talk and another who seemed to blame me for everything that went wrong. Now that we were no longer in an emergency, we had fallen into an uncomfortable silence. To top it all off, we were lost.

I drooped over Kir's neck and let my hair fall forward while a few tears coursed down my cheeks. One day. One measly day and I was ready to give up! I couldn't believe I was that much of a wimp. I didn't offer Kir any direction, but he started walking again, and I didn't protest.

I was grateful that Imishi stayed silent. I didn't bother to look up while Kir plodded along, up and down low hills. The air cooled, and somewhere nearby birds were singing. I must have lost track of time. Kir finally came to a halt and stamped his feet. I looked up.

The sun was setting. We were in a flat area dotted with pools of clear water that gave off a faint aquamarine glow in the fading sunlight. On the far side of the pools, a dense stand of trees formed a sheltering half circle. Low, thick grass covered the ground between and around the pools.

An image rose in my mind: Kir resting and riderless. The image was clear, but with blurry edges, as if I were looking through a tunnel made of fog.

"Kir would like us to get off his back," I said.

I let Imishi dismount first, her feet touching the ground as lightly as a feather. My own dismount was more clumsy, because I was so stiff and sore.

"How do you know he wanted us to get off his back?" Imishi asked.

"He told me." Picking up a new image from Kir, I removed the saddlebags and blanket. Kir shook himself, whinnied, then walked over to a pool and began to drink.

Imishi made a skeptical sound. "The horses of Kib Valley do not speak in words. I often understand what my cousin wants, but only because I have known him so long. Do you claim to understand Kir's language?"

"Not exactly." Then I explained, as much as I could, about the emotions and images that I could pick up from Kir's mind and how I had figured out what was bothering the marsh troll. When Imishi actually looked impressed, I told her about my rapport with stray animals in the waking world. I wondered if I would be able to sense their feelings when I got home, like I could sense Kir's in Aventurine.

I sat down on the grass, which was soft and springy. It felt amazing to lie back on it. I had to force myself to sit up and remove my boots. "We might as well have supper and spend the night here," I said.

"Did Kir tell you that, too?"

"No, but he's making himself at home, we don't have any flashlights, and we could all use some rest. So I just figured it was a good idea," I said. "And I need some time to work on my map, plus I'm starving."

"We should get clean first," Imishi said, picking up the horse blanket, which was caked with mud from the swamp. She dipped the blanket in the pool nearest her, just once. As she pulled the material out of the water, dirt streamed away until it was clean. The fairy girl took a step back from the pool and shook the blanket so that it snapped in the warm evening air. "The magic of Willowood cloth," Imishi said, showing it to me.

The cloth was dirt free and completely dry!

I went to a pool close to the ones Imishi and Kir were using. I dipped a toe into the water, which was just cool enough to be refreshing. Throwing caution to the wind, I jumped in, fully clothed, and ducked my head under the water. After the swamp, with its murky water and moldy smells, this was absolute heaven.

I surfaced, rubbed my hands over my skin to remove any lingering traces of mud, dunked my head again, and swished my hair around. I got out of the pool feeling clean and revived. I removed several articles of clothing, shook them out to dry them, then dressed again. It was the most fun I'd ever had doing laundry.

We gathered for dinner, eating the food from the Willowood Fairies, except for Kir, who munched on mouthfuls of grass. After supper, Imishi found what she called a cinder oak and broke off a glowing twig that I could use for light while working on my map. She dug into the saddlebags as I worked.

"Look, Zally!" Imishi said.

I glanced up, and by the light of the twig, I saw that she was holding a silver comb. "Pretty," I said, looking back at my map.

Imishi started humming and I looked up again. She was combing her coral hair. Then she took a narrow section, wrapped it around one finger, and made a swirling motion from the root to the tip. As she twirled her finger, slender tendrils of vines grew around the strand in a spiral. Miniature yellow flowers blossomed on the vines. The comb was pretty, but this was enchanting.

Malia and her parents took me to a Renaissance fair once in New Jersey. There had been a booth where you could get your hair braided into lots of little braids and decorated with flowers. But it had been too expensive, so we had just watched for a long time. I watched now, my map forgotten, as Imishi repeated the process until her hair was held back in a dozen flowery hair vines.

"How did you do that?" I asked.

Imishi smiled. "I could do the same with your hair," she offered.

"Really?" I asked.

Imishi nodded, her grin growing.

"I'd love that. But would I have to take them out to sleep?" I asked.

"No, hair vines are very comfortable to sleep in, and they don't tangle. You can keep your hair like this for days. It keeps your hair out of your eyes, too."

I wasn't about to turn her down. "Can I work on the map while you do it?" I asked.

Imishi nodded again. "That is a good idea. That way no time is wasted."

So while Imishi twisted my long hair into vines, I let my mind follow its inspiration to sketch the next part of the map. When we finished, we were both in a much better mood than we had been earlier at the swamp.

"We'd better get some sleep now," I said, looking at the terrain on my newly drawn map. "We're going to have some hard traveling tomorrow."

Kir looked up and snorted.

As I put away the map and the quill, Imishi folded her wings carefully behind her, curled up with her head on the saddlebags, and fell instantly to sleep, snoring very gently. I covered her with Kir's blanket and smiled at her. Maybe she wasn't so bad after all.

I put my head on the other side of the saddlebags and tried to sleep. The sky filled with stars as I watched. The constellations were different from what I was used to, and the stars were brighter than any I had ever seen. I fell asleep wondering what stories the fairies told about their constellations.

I woke up to Kir snuffling in my hair. Imishi was already up and had put out breakfast for us, including fresh water in what looked like bark cups. The sky was pinky gold.

"So you know which way we're headed today?" Imishi asked as I ate an eggy pastry.

"Let me look at the map," I said.

Imishi handed me my woven bag and I took out the map. We looked at it together, Imishi brushing the crumbs from my pastry off of it.

One of the coolest things about my map of Aventurine was the way parts of the map would expand to show us close-ups of the areas we were going through. When we left a region, it would shrink again, leaving more room on the map to see where we were at the time. In that way, it was like a map on a Web site.

One of the *not*-cool things about the map was the way it didn't really prepare you for where you were going. You could plan part of the way, but not a whole trip. Although I wondered if perhaps there was a way it would be able to show someone more. . . . If I saw Queen Patchouli again, if I succeeded in my quest, I would ask.

I traced a finger along the trail we had taken from the marsh, to the comfortable haven where we had spent the night. I closed my eyes, my fingers on the map. I felt that there were more obstacles before the valley, but I had drawn only one thing so far on the way: three trees and a couple of random plants I didn't recognize. I couldn't tell by the drawing whether we were about to reach three trees, an orchard, a bonsai garden of miniature shrubs, or a forest.

"That's the way," I said to Imishi.

"I'll pack up," she said.

She folded everything carefully and stored it all in the saddlebags. Kir found a large rock for her to stand on so she could lift the saddlebags onto his back.

I was amazed at Imishi's change in attitude. She didn't seem angry at me anymore. Could something as simple as fixing my hair have made the change? Maybe my genuine appreciation had helped. Or that we had seen each other as girls, both liking pretty things, enjoying something simple outside of the daunting quest before us. In any case, our cheerfulness made that daunting quest less scary and more exciting.

It was a good thing I was feeling that way, because as it turned out, our path ran through a *jungle*—and by "path," I don't really mean any kind of real road or trail; it was more like narrow corridors between trees, shrubs, and ground cover. Kir could just set his feet down without tripping over vines and branches, and Imishi and I could barely sit upright on Kir's back and not get smacked in the face by springy palm fronds.

One of the definitions of "jungle" is land that is overgrown with tangled masses of tropical vegetation. This jungle was no exception. It looked very much like pictures my parents have shown me of the jungles of Guatemala.

Plants of every shape and size grew there—trees hundreds of feet tall with countless leafy branches, ferns higher than our heads, thick clusters of bamboo, creeping ground cover that grew between and around the tree trunks, flowers in all colors and scents, and vines dangling from branches high above. The hot air was heavy with moisture, and the light that filtered down through the leaves was tinged a faint green. The smells of the jungle were rich and damp.

Imishi kept her wings folded tightly out of the way to prevent them from being poked or further damaged by the plants we were passing through. We both stayed alert. Watching Kir's ears swivel this way and that, I knew he was keeping alert, too.

"I wish I could have flown over this," Imishi sighed. I didn't hear any whininess or criticism in her tone, just wistfulness.

I could feel Kir's worry for his sire as we rode on. It was a constant reminder of our need to hurry. We continued in silence for an hour or so. Of course the jungle is anything but silent: birds chirped, twittered, and cawed; frogs croaked; monkeys chattered; water dripped; insects buzzed or clicked; leaves rustled.

The jungle was filled with amazing sights, but it was what I couldn't see that began to trouble me. I'm not sure when I became aware of it, but I sensed a new restlessness from Kir. Animals have instincts to tell them when something big is about to happen, like a thunderstorm or an earthquake. So I thought maybe Kir was picking up something like that. The answer slammed into my thoughts a moment later: a feeling so strong that it overpowered my connection with Kir for a moment. A creature was somewhere near us—a creature filled with a wild hunger.

Pushing the thought away, I cleared my mind. I reached out to Kir and directed him to go faster along the path that, according to my map, would take us out of the jungle.

Imishi felt the change. "What's wrong, why don't we—"

I held up a hand to caution her to silence. I turned, with a finger pressed to my lips. She went quiet and started looking around more carefully. I had the creepiest feeling that we were being watched.

Kir picked his way through the trees and underbrush faster than I had thought possible. We broke through the jungle into an open area filled with ruins. My mouth must have dropped open. Some of the ancient buildings looked like step pyramids. Others were little more than foundations raised above the ground with steps leading up to the flat area. The whole scene reminded me of pictures that decorate the walls of our bakery—Mayan ruins like Chichén Itzá, Tikal, and Caracol.

I turned and saw Imishi looking around as wide-eyed as I felt. I nudged Kir forward, and I got a blast of the hunger feeling again. We passed a couple of foot-high circular walls with carvings of horses, wild-cats, birds, and monkeys on them. I peeked into one circle and saw that it was a well. Another appeared to be a shallow fire pit. I wondered if we could hide somewhere here.

I heard a low, rumbling growl from the trees behind us.

Finally I saw what I was looking for: a small domed building made of brown stone blocks set upon a raised foundation. I pointed it out to my companions. The square structure, except for part of the ceiling and a chink here and there, was largely intact. A steep grassy slope led up one side of the raised foundation, and Kir started toward it. There was a sudden shriek and flutter as something zoomed past my head—a brightly colored parrot flying toward the same stone structure.

Suddenly I started to see animals everywhere around us—some on the ground, some on pyramids, a few floating in the air. Not real, solid animals, but transparent and hazy, like mirages. *Or ghosts.*

Then I heard a snarl and a roar.

Kir didn't need any encouragement; he ran at full

gallop up the slope onto the raised foundation. Imishi and I stayed on with the help of the magical blanket. The square building, about the size of a large gazebo, was directly ahead of us. Dead leaves and vines littered the ground. At each side of the building—at least the sides I could see—I noticed traces of faint stone circles.

Barely slowing, Kir jumped all the way over one of the stone circles. We came down hard on the other side. Imishi nearly squashed me against Kir's neck on landing, and both of us were winded. Kir didn't wait for us to recover. Finding an opening into the building that was barely wide enough to admit a horse, he squeezed through, while Imishi and I kept our heads ducked down to keep from hitting them as we entered the building. As soon as we were inside, we were able to sit up again and saw that the domed ceiling was at least twenty-five feet high.

Ignoring my sore muscles, I swung off Kir's back and started to search around for something to block the entrance.

"There's a door here," Imishi said, hopping down beside me and starting to push on a flat block of stone by the entrance that was the same size and shape as the opening we had squeezed through. She was right.

I helped Imishi push, and the slab started to move.

There was a sharp squawk overhead, and a harsh voice screamed, "We're here, we're here!"

The parrot! Was it inside with us?

Another, louder roar echoed around us. I pushed harder, and the door moved a little more. Kir backed up toward us, pressed his rear against the door, and shoved backward. Just as the door closed, I caught a glimpse of something outside—tawny fur spotted with black.

A jaguar, bigger than any jaguar I'd ever seen. It was as tall as Kir!

Panting and shaking, I slid to the floor, which felt pleasantly cool after the humid jungle heat. Imishi, tucking her wings up out of the way, sat beside me. With a noisy flutter, the parrot flew down from a hole in the ceiling to perch on the saddle blanket atop Kir's back.

For a chamber with no electricity, our refuge was surprisingly bright. Slits and square openings in the walls and a hole in the dome let enough sunlight in to illuminate the room. It was obvious that we weren't going to be leaving until we were sure the jaguar was gone, so we ate some of our rations and opened one of the pods of water.

The parrot amused itself, walking around on the floor of the chamber, eating any crumbs we dropped, and squawking, "More for me, more for me!" I tried to ignore it.

After we ate, Imishi and I peered out various wall slits and saw the jungle cat prowling in slow circles around our building. I got goose bumps each time the jaguar's mind brushed against mine, and I felt its hunger. I caught a glimpse of its eyes. They glowed jade green, giving me the eerie feeling that the jaguar could see us. Its gaze never left the building. The cat must have weighed hundreds of pounds; it would have been ridiculous to think that we could just outrun it or overpower it somehow. No, we would have to wait and hope it found some other prey in the jungle. Once or twice I thought I saw other animals out there—just a glimmer, and then they were gone.

The room was not as small as I had first thought. With each wall about twice as long as Kir was from nose to rump, and with the sunlight helping to make the room feel less claustrophobic, there were much worse places we could have been trapped. My eyes traveled upward to the domed ceiling. I thought that at night there would be a wonderful view of the stars through the opening. Then it occurred to me what the little building reminded me of: an observatory. I'd even seen pictures of ancient Mayan observatories, some square, some round. I looked at the sunlight-dappled walls around us, and for the first time I realized that each side of the room was carved.

"I wish we could leave," Imishi said.

I could feel that Kir was anxious about the wasted time as well. Even though we were safe for the moment, we weren't getting any closer to Kib Valley.

As best I could tell, three walls held carvings of the building we were in, surrounded by the sun and moon and stars and thousands of animals. Each carving also showed animal constellations outlined in the stars. Whoever had lived here clearly loved animals.

Imishi pointed to the wall nearest her. "Did you know there is writing here? And something else I believe will interest you. I think you should see it for yourself."

I went over to see the writing Imishi was talking about. Beneath the text was a separate carving of a creature with feathers—a dragon? I wondered. Each culture seems to have different legends and various

images of such creatures. Chinese dragons tend to be long and snaky, whereas European paintings of dragons remind me of small dinosaurs with batlike wings. This creature was more like drawings of feathered serpents of Maya and Aztec lore, and it had been singled out as special from the host of animals in the other carvings.

I looked at the writing above the carved serpent.

Kir nosed between us and looked at the wall.

"The feathered snake is called Kukulkan," Imishi said, reading along with me. "According to the carved legend, it was wise beyond all other creatures, fearsome when angered, and could fly with the speed of an arrow."

The golden horse gave an uneasy snort.

Below the image of the snake was an even more intricate carving that took my breath away: a map! I studied it, reaching out a hand to trace the lines. *This* was what the city had looked like long ago, before it was ruined.

"*¡Ay, mira!* Thank you, Imishi. It's—"

"Of course!" Imishi interrupted, her face filled with wonder. "I should have realized it before. This is Ool-Kib. It was a Kib fairy city, abandoned in ancient times when a volcano destroyed much of it. Since then, the spirits of innocent creatures have been drawn here after they die."

The parrot took that opportunity to stretch its wings and fly through the hole in the ceiling. It then circled the observatory, squawking, "We're here, we're here!"

"Stupid bird!" I muttered in exasperation. I peeked through one of the wall slits but saw neither the bird nor the jaguar. Outside, though, I heard a menacing growl and a snarl, followed by several frantic shrieks from the parrot, some loud snapping sounds like branches breaking, a split second of silence, and then—

A terrible roar echoed through the room where we stood.

7

The Innocent

The jaguar's hungry roar echoed in the stone chamber. I quickly scanned the small room for any sign of the jungle cat, but our little band of travelers was still alone. It was obvious that none of the holes in the walls or ceiling could possibly be large enough to admit the cat. The door was still closed. Yet the rumble of the cat breathing in and out sounded so close.

Imishi jumped onto Kir's back. She leaned forward with her arms around his neck, her wings spread flat, to protect him. It probably wouldn't have helped, had the jaguar actually been in the room with us, but it showed her courage.

From Kir, I felt the same worry as before: concern for his sire and the rest of Kib Valley. He knew the jaguar was not in the room with us. So why did the roaring suddenly seem so loud? I peeked through the slits one after another but could not catch a glimpse of the jaguar.

From outside I heard, "We're here, we're here, we're here!" The parrot was not dead, then. I smiled as the fleeting thought reminded me of a Monty Python DVD my oldest brother, Ed, sometimes watched—something silly about a dead parrot. It seemed *our* parrot was safe, though, and hadn't been eaten by the jaguar.

I saw no sign of the jaguar outside, but I could hear her and feel her. (I could tell it was female now.) Strangely, I no longer felt *hunger* in the thoughts of the wild creature; instead came a feeling of fear and being trapped. The parrot called, "Safe now, safe now!" I wondered if the bird had any idea what it was saying. It was possible. I wondered if I could try thinking to it myself.

Kir whinnied.

Imishi sat up on his back. "What can you see?"

"Not much," I admitted. "Just the jungle and our parrot friend. But I feel something, and I need to check it out." I went to the door and grasped the heavy metal ring that was affixed to the stone slab where I would normally expect a doorknob to be. I pulled and the door swung inward just enough so I could squeeze out.

"Zally, no—it's too dangerous!" Imishi cried.

"Close the door behind me," I whispered back. "I'll be okay." I heard the scraping of stone as Imishi shut the door. Staying close to the small building, I inched to the corner and peeked around it. At the edge of my vision I caught a glimpse of something—the jaguar? No, it was just a ghostly animal spirit of some sort.

I slid along the wall, taking care not to step into the stone circle of grass and leaves on that side of the building. If Kir had not wanted to step into it, neither did I. At the next corner, I peeked around again: no jaguar.

I turned the corner and began inching along the wall. Something was different here: the stone circle, which was wider than I was tall, was not completely filled in with grass and debris. A sound came from it, like an echoey, raspy bark. The parrot—minus a few green tail feathers—fluttered down to perch on one of the low encircling stones. "We're here, we're here! Safe now, safe now!"

"Shhh!" I hissed, sending a thought of silence to it at the same time.

The parrot stopped squawking and continued bobbing his head and shifting his weight as if he were doing a dance. It seemed I was really talking to animals! I wished I could celebrate how cool this was, but this wasn't the time.

I noticed a jagged hole in the surface closest to the building. About a third of the ground inside the circle had broken away and fallen inward. I knelt beside the parrot, leaned forward, and looked into the hole. It was a deep pit, more than twenty feet down, and the jaguar was at the bottom.

Turning her glowing eyes upward, the jaguar saw me. I didn't sense any threat from her, but she crouched and sprang upward. I gasped and jerked back. I heard the jaguar's claws scrabble on the hard, smooth stone at the side of the pit for a moment before she fell back with a raspy growl of feline frustration.

I saw now that the ground inside the circle was nothing more than a thin crust of dried clay covered with dirt, pebbles, leaves, and twigs to disguise it.

"Safe now," the bird squawked again.

I was getting the idea that the parrot really did know what he was saying, albeit with a limited vocabulary. "Okay, okay," I said. "But what am I supposed to do?" I leaned over and peered down into the hole again. This time when the jaguar saw me, I felt a flicker of . . . what? Hope? The jaguar's thoughts and feelings were edged with green. I drew back again and looked through one of the slits into the building. I almost laughed out loud when I saw one fairy eye and one horse eye staring back at me.

"It's okay, you can come out now," I said. "Just don't step in any of those stone circles."

A minute later, Kir and Imishi joined me. I had not moved from beside the pit, and I found myself wondering why Kir's instincts had steered him clear of the pit when the jaguar's had not. I felt a strange sensation in my mind as Kir tried to explain something about the way vibrations in the ground had warned him that there was a hollow area ahead. I gave a mental shrug. Maybe the jaguar had been distracted by stalking us—or by that loud parrot.

"We need to go now," Imishi said, mounting up. "We have lost much time."

I nodded and stood, still staring into the pit, brushing dirt from my knees. Imishi stretched out a hand to help me up onto Kir's back. Something stopped me. Feelings tingled and poked at my mind: discouragement, disappointment, despair, tinged green at the edges.

"We have to help her get out of the pit," I said.

Imishi stared at me, her face going pale with disbelief. "*What?* We just spent hours escaping that beast, and now you want to *help* it?"

When she put it that way, it did sound like a pretty dumb thing to do. But something told me that this was the *right* thing to do. Kir neighed and took a step backward. I gave my friends an apologetic look. "I know, I know. I'm sorry, but I have to do this. She won't try to hurt us now."

Imishi snorted. "It is a *jaguar*! That's what they *do*—hunt and eat other creatures!"

"She needs help, or she'll die," I said. "Isn't that what you Kib Fairies do—help other creatures?"

The fairy girl's eyes narrowed, and she shook her head. "Not creatures that want to eat us! We're wasting time, and we need to get back to help Queen Carmina and creatures who *deserve* our help!" She threaded her fingers through Kir's mane, and he turned to face the jungle. I knew that they wouldn't leave without me. So did they.

I went back to the hole, eased myself down onto my stomach, and stuck my head over the edge. The jaguar's paws were flecked with blood, as if she had been clawing at the walls. When she saw me, I felt a flicker of anticipation, of pleading. Was that possible? The jaguar crouched and tried to leap again, but this time the leap took her barely halfway up the walls before she fell back to the ground. She turned in agitation, lashing her tail. I saw that the bottom of the pit was littered with the bones of creatures that had not escaped.

I stared down at the jaguar, trying to catch her eerie gaze, doing my best to send her a message. Our eyes locked, and the jaguar stopped pacing. Focusing on the jade glow, I sent thoughts to her as best I could, thoughts like *calm* and *friendly* and *rescue.*

The cat sat on her haunches, staring up at me. I sent her thoughts: *We are your friends. We are not food.* I wondered if the concept of friendship was one the jaguar could even understand, but it seemed to work. She lay down on the floor of the pit, surrounded by bones, and only the tip of her tail twitched. I could tell she was ready to wait patiently for help.

I stuck my head further through the hole to look around. A couple of my long hair vines slid forward into the hole to dangle beside my face. The jaguar, seeing this, raised a paw slightly, as if to bat at my hair vines—reminding me of one of the kittens playing with the shoestring. My hair dangled only a couple of feet into the hole, but it gave me an idea.

Wait, I thought to the jaguar. *I'll be back.*

She lowered her paw and rested her chin on it.

I got up, then spoke to Kir and Imishi. "Look, I'm really sorry. I know you don't understand this part of my quest. But the jaguar in that pit is an innocent, and I have to help her. Now, the two of you can either wait however long it takes me to do this by myself, or you can decide to help me and we can all get out of here that much sooner."

With that, I marched away across the foundation and down the one grassy slope to the edge of the jungle. The apparitions of two mice scampered along beside me. I knew what I needed, and I had to find just the right one. I did not look back, but it wasn't long before I heard the soft thud of Kir's hooves on the grass behind me. That was a relief. It only took a minute or two to find what I was searching for: a tall, fallen stalk of bamboo about as big around as my waist. A bunch of small, leafy branches sprouted from the fat stalk. It didn't look too large, yet it looked strong enough. I tried to pick up one end. The bamboo was surprisingly heavy—perhaps it wasn't bamboo after all.

I turned to look at my friends. "Could you help me get this over to the hole, please?"

Imishi got a strange look on her face. Then she jumped off Kir's back, patted his flank, and said, "You will be doing most of the work, cousin." Kir nodded his understanding.

Imishi rummaged through the saddlebags and drew out a length of silken ribbon. She unrolled it and, holding each end in one hand, placed the end of the loop under her foot to hold it still. She smoothed the ribbon with her hands, and the ends grew longer and longer. Concentrating, she folded the ends several times, crossing them over each other. Her hands moved so fast they were almost a blur as she wove the narrow ribbon to create a sort of mesh net with a large hole at the center and two long trailing ends of ribbon.

Moving to Kir, she threw the open part of the loop over his head and pulled it down to his shoulders. Then I understood: Imishi had made a harness. She smoothed out the two ends of the ribbon until they were long enough to reach the bamboo stalk and tied them securely around it. It was nothing short of brilliant, and done in less than five minutes.

Imishi and I tied the bamboo with the ribbons. Kir did not need me to tell him what to do when we finished. He took a few steps forward until he felt the weight of the bamboo on the harness. Then he leaned into the harness and tried to walk, but the load was too heavy. Imishi and I pushed the bamboo from behind. It budged. Slightly.

All of a sudden a herd of translucent golden horses appeared around us.

"The horses of Kib Valley!" Imishi gasped.

"Their spirits are helping us save the jaguar."

Kir whinnied a surprised greeting to his ancestors, who responded in a ghostly, musical echo. Then a shimmer surged out from them into Kir and Imishi, growing brighter until the whole group radiated a dazzling golden light. A feeling of elation flowed from all of them into me as well.

Imishi lifted one end of the heavy bamboo. At the other end, Kir took powerful steps, pulling the stalk forward with his harness. Surrounded by the brilliant spirits, we headed up the grassy slope toward the observatory.

Picking up a short length of branch from the ground, I ran ahead to the pit and broke out the rest of the clay surface inside the stone circle. When Kir arrived, dragging the bamboo all the way to the edge of the pit, I was ready. Strengthened by the horse spirits, Imishi and Kir positioned the stalk so that the largest portion of it rested on the stone rim of the pit. Then I untied the fairy-silk rope from the bamboo and released Kir from his harness. Dipping their heads, the glowing herd of horses backed away from the stone circle but did not leave us.

I looked down into the pit, still radiating calmness and friendship toward the jaguar. In my mind I created an image of the jaguar moving to the edge of the pit nearest me. Her thoughts came back to me, trusting, reassured . . . and wild. She did as I asked.

When Imishi, Kir, and I lined up on the same side of the bamboo and started to push, rolling it in the direction of the pit, I felt a brief moment of hesitation—we were about to release a dangerous creature. I quickly dismissed the thought. This was the right thing to do.

We rolled the stalk a couple of feet before one end went over the edge, tilted, and slid down into the hole, taking the rest of the bamboo with it. I glanced down inside to see that the bottom end of the bamboo had landed firmly at one edge of the pit. The top was wedged against the other side, just below the top edge of the pit where I stood. Knowing that the jaguar could take it from there, Imishi, Kir, and I stepped back into the herd of spirit horses.

"Thank you, cousins," Imishi said while Kir whinnied his gratitude and I bowed.

Together, the spirit herd reared in a joyful salute and then galloped away.

Imishi and I mounted Kir, and we headed back to our proper path through the jungle. Spirits of animals flickered all around us.

Just before we entered the dense foliage again, something approached from behind in a flurry.

Startled, I turned to see that the parrot had landed behind Imishi on the fairy-silk blanket between the saddlebags.

"Here we are, here we are!"

I smiled. He was a bit of a pest, but the bird seemed to have become attached to us. I saw no harm in his coming along on our journey, since I didn't seem to have a choice.

From the corner of my eye, I saw the jaguar emerge from the pit, up on the foundation outside the observatory. The glowing gaze searched—and found me.

Imishi saw where I was looking and said, "Let's go, before it comes after us."

I sighed, knowing she still didn't understand why I had released the jaguar. "Just because something is dangerous doesn't mean it's not an innocent," I pointed out. "And helping innocents is part of my quest."

Imishi didn't look at me. "That is not *my* quest," she said quietly.

I turned and faced forward again. As we rode back into the jungle, I knew I had done the right thing. And every so often, I could still feel a whisper of the wild jaguar mind.

• • •

As it turned out, the rest of the way through the jungle was not as overgrown as the inward path had been. We crossed a brook, and at one point Kir made a brief detour to avoid a long, fat snake hanging in front of us from a tree.

A few minutes later, a trio of spider monkeys dropped fruit from a branch above us and screeched with laughter when one of the fruits hit my head. It didn't hurt, but the monkeys were annoying. When they threw the next projectile, I was ready—and caught it in midair. Imishi took the fruit, cut it up with her shell knife, handed me a wedge, and gave a small chunk to the parrot behind her.

I took several bites, gave the monkeys a mock bow, said, "Thank you!" and sent them a vague idea that it was impolite to throw fruit. I'm not sure what they made of the thoughts I sent—but they did stop dropping things on us and simply swung through the trees above our heads from then on.

After that, I kept getting the feeling that someone or something was watching us from behind. I shook myself, trying to get the thought out of my head.

Behind me, Imishi said, "Ow. Ow—OW!"

I turned instantly, afraid some animal had chomped her arm as we'd ridden by. It was just the parrot perched atop the fairy's head.

"He walked up my back with his talons!" she exclaimed.

I made sure to hold my smile until I was faced forward again.

Equally unconcerned, Kir continued onward.

"Safe now!" the bird squawked merrily.

I turned to give the parrot a stern look. He bobbed slightly but easily kept his balance, since he was grasping one of Imishi's hair vines with both claws. "Listen, bird," I said, "uh . . . I'm going to call you Monty from now on, okay? Anyway, Monty, you can't just walk all over people and hurt them. If you want to stay with us, you need to become part of our team and not cause problems, understand?"

He bobbed his head.

I sent him as clear a picture as I could of him moving to Imishi's shoulder and sitting still. "And don't dig your claws into her," I added. As I said it, Monty hopped onto Imishi's shoulder. Talking to animals was awesome; I hoped with all my heart that it was a skill that wouldn't go away when I woke up at home.

We continued in contented silence until we left the jungle entirely. Waving good-bye to the spider monkeys, Imishi said, "Do you know where we are, or should we stop so you can map some more?"

I tried to feel the pull of which direction to go next. I couldn't, so we took a short rest to give me time to sketch a couple more areas on the map. Because it had fascinated me and seemed good for the general purpose of mapping Aventurine, I quickly drew the area of Ool-Kib I had seen on the observatory wall. After that, I let my eyes unfocus and my mind drift. It didn't take long to lose myself in a sketching trance, my hand just going by itself. When I finished and looked up, the sun was still high overhead.

"Done already?" Imishi asked.

I smiled and ran my finger across the map to show her where we were going. "Yes, I think this is all of it." I pointed to a hill and said, "Kib Valley should be just beyond this. It shouldn't take us more than a day."

Imishi's face lit up at that. Monty hopped onto my shoulder, eyed my drawing, and tapped his beak on a spot right next to my picture of the jungle. "We're here, we're here!"

"Be careful with that!" I said, shooing him away, rolling up the map, and putting it back into my bag.

We set off again in the direction of the hill. The ground became hard and uneven, strewn with sharp black rocks, some of which came up to Kir's withers. Kir had to step carefully to avoid being cut by them. It occurred to me as the ground began to slope upward that a topographical map would be useful, too. I wondered if there was a way to make the map display in three dimensions.

The parrot took wing, flying ahead, then circling back. When he landed on Imishi's shoulder again, she had a sad look on her face, as if she was reminded of her inability to fly.

"Up we go, up we go!" Monty squawked.

Sure enough, the ground got steeper. I groaned, knowing where I had seen pictures of this type of terrain before: in my atlases, in the sections about Central America and the South Pacific. This was volcanic terrain, which meant that the little hill I had drawn on the map was most likely a volcano—a volcano we had to go past, or even over.

"I hope this isn't what I think it is," I muttered to myself.

We took another quick rest. Monty hopped onto a rock and stood, shifting from foot to foot again. He whistled and squawked happily. All of a sudden, a squawk turned into a screech. I looked over to see a green and brown lizard scurrying away, its mouth full of parrot feathers. The reptile must have been over three feet long! Had it been trying to eat Monty and gotten scared away?

Monty launched into the air, but his balance had been thrown off (from lack of tail feathers, maybe), and he didn't get far. He fluttered downward and tried to land on Kir's back but only managed to grasp the fairy-silk blanket with one claw. He dangled upside down, flopping and screeching.

I jumped to my feet to help, stifling a laugh.

Imishi got there first. I said soothing things to Monty, reinforcing the words with my thoughts, while Imishi untangled his foot from the blanket, turned him upright again, and gently set him on her shoulder once more. He shook himself and looked at both of us through slitted eyes.

"He's going to pretend it didn't happen," I whispered to Imishi, and she laughed. Kir snorted in a laughing way as well, and Monty turned around on Imishi's shoulder and didn't look at us. This of course only made us all laugh more. Laughing felt great. We got going again, feeling happy.

I figured we could make it as far as the hill by

nightfall. After a few hours, I asked Kir if he could find us a spot like the one where we had spent the previous night, with protection and plenty of water, so we could get a good night's sleep before we made our approach to Kib Valley. He found a place where the rock was smoother and dipped downward for fifty yards or so, leading to a cave in the rock wall. Beside this, water trickled through a groove in the wall like a miniature waterfall, forming a shallow pool no wider than my outstretched arms.

We headed down to the cave, Kir setting his hooves carefully to avoid slipping on the smoother rock. I had a sudden fiercely protective feeling—blurred at the edges—and realized the feeling wasn't coming from me. Before we could get to the shelter, a bizarre creature landed in front of us. I had never seen anything like it, except in a carving.

It was a giant snake, bigger around than Kir and about five times as long—a snake with feathers.

8

The Thief

"Who dares to steal from the fearsome and mighty Kukulkan?" the voice of the serpent boomed. The velvety sound poured through the air around us like liquid thunder.

The serpent's body was covered with scales in shades of silver and metallic charcoal. There were three separate feathery wreaths along its coils in a rainbow of colors. When the creature raised half of its body into the air to glower down at us, the wreaths of feathers split and formed three pairs of wings. The serpent breathed down on us with a hiss.

Imishi sat straight and still behind me. I could tell Kir badly wanted to retreat but held his ground out of loyalty to us. But here's an incredible thing. After falling into a swamp, being attacked by clouds of insects, worrying about dying innocents, and being stalked by a jaguar, I wasn't afraid. I wasn't surprised that "the fearsome and mighty Kukulkan" could talk, either.

It sounds crazy, but what I felt most at that instant was *fascinated*. I cleared my throat and said, "We are honored to meet you, Kukulkan. We are friends of Queen Carmina, on our way to Kib Valley. May we rest here?"

The serpent moved its head back and forth, its feathery wings rippling. "Thieves are not friends. Thieves do not rest."

"Not thieves, not thieves!" Monty croaked weakly.

I could not imagine *what* the feathered serpent thought we had stolen. We hadn't even had any water yet. Other than that, I could see nothing in any direction that one of us might want, much less try to take.

"Thieves!" the serpent repeated. "You stole my only!"

Searching my mind for a way to answer, I felt a rush of emotions from the serpent: sorrow, protectiveness, and outrage.

"Not thieves. We *are* friends," I said, with as much confidence as I could muster while looking at a forty-foot-long dragony creature. "If we help you find what was stolen, will you let us sleep here?"

The serpent sighed, blowing a gust of hot air on us. "You will help me find my very own Egg?"

"Your egg is lost?" I asked.

The serpent hissed, "Yessss."

"Of course we will help you!" Imishi said stoutly.

Kir whinnied enthusiastically, and Monty bobbed up and down, squawking, "Find the egg, find the egg!"

I wasn't sure what to do. We had just reached the base of a volcano that was probably riddled with crevices and caves—plenty of places that a thief could hide an egg, *if* the thief hadn't taken the egg somewhere else entirely or eaten it.

"What happened?" I asked Kukulkan. "How long has the egg been missing?"

The serpent mother sorrowfully shook her head. "I went to sleep here. In the morning, Egg was gone."

"Do any of you have ideas?" I asked, turning to the others.

"Find the egg!" Monty repeated helpfully.

Kir gave a gentle snort and sent an image of the night sky, reminding me that it would soon be dark.

Hesitating, Imishi said, "Could you—could you draw a map, perhaps?"

I stared at her in surprise. It was certainly worth a try. I pulled the roll of map paper out of my bag, along with my quill pen. I calmly explained to Kukulkan what I was trying to do.

I thought that if I could touch the feathered serpent while working, I might feel some connection with the egg that would help. The serpent gradually lowered herself until she was lying flat on the ground. I sat by her on the rock floor, spread out a fresh map page, and leaned back against her. Her skin was smooth and muscley, not at all slippery. I opened my thoughts to hers and let her worry touch me. The quill, still loaded with cacao ink, seemed to spring to life in my hand. I was soon sketching.

When my map was finished, I stared at it. It showed a glowing orange hole halfway up the volcano where the egg was now. Kir carried Imishi and me while I directed, Monty rode on Imishi's shoulder, and Kukulkan—her wings beating as fast as a hummingbird's—hovered along beside us. Kir made good speed up the rock slope despite the waning light. Before darkness fell completely, however, Kukulkan drew a deep breath, held it for a moment, then exhaled a ball of green fire that hovered in midair and followed us to light our way.

Half an hour later, we reached the cave to which my map led us. Unfortunately, its mouth was only a few feet high, too small to allow the feathered serpent or Kir inside. So Imishi and I agreed to search if we could take the green fire with us. Kukulkan gladly sent it through the opening ahead of us. We ducked and followed it into the cave. Monty stayed on the fairy girl's shoulder.

The green light lifted itself toward the high cavern ceiling. Before long, Monty began squawking and screaming one word over and over: "Thief, thief!" Hopping down, he scrabbled along the cave floor.

Exchanging surprised glances, Imishi and I hurried after him. When we caught up with Monty, he was perched on a short stalagmite above a scooped-out area in the cave floor that formed a sort of nest—complete with one copper-shelled egg the size of a football. I leaned down to pick it up.

A deep voice reverberated in the cavern. "Who dares to disturb the fearsome and mighty Kukulkan?"

Imishi and I gaped at each other in shock. Could it be true? Could there really be another Kukulkan?

"Thief, thief!" Monty squawked again, then zoomed to dive-bomb something on the floor of the cavern. The green ball of fire moved to shed its light on the area.

"No, you shall not look upon me!" the voice boomed. "All who challenge the glorious Kukulkan are doomed! Flee for your lives!" The voice became more frantic.

We looked at the ceiling and walls, behind rocks, trying to find where the voice was coming from. Monty squawked and swooped at the thing on the floor again. The grand voice boomed once more, "Flee! Fl—" but this time it cut off in a strangled yelp, accompanied by a thundering *Squawwwk!*

"Monty?!" Imishi cried.

Monty's squawk had exploded through the walls at the same moment that he had swooped, and something had made his voice sound louder. I went closer to see what he had found. Monty's claws were firmly wrapped around the tail of a plump lizard a few feet long. I couldn't tell what kind of lizard, because its head was hidden in a hole in the cavern wall.

The green ball of light hovered closer to show us more. The neck and shoulders of the lizard sprouted a variety of mismatched feathers that seemed to be stuck on with gooey sap. Several of the emerald green feathers were a perfect match to Monty's stolen tail feathers. Without needing to be asked, Imishi grasped the tail and helped Monty pull while I took the shoulders and legs to extract the lizard's head from the hole in the wall. We succeeded almost immediately, and I blocked the hole with the toe of my boot so the lizard could not stick its head back in. A boom echoed through the chamber.

The lizard, which looked like an oversized iguana, except for its shiny green-brown skin and the feathers glued to it, reared back and said, "Beware the wrath of the powerful Kukulkan. Flee, flee!" But the voice was tiny, high, and almost funny.

My brothers and I used to watch *The Wizard of Oz* together every Thanksgiving, and this situation reminded me of the scene where Toto pulls aside the curtain on the man pretending to be the wizard. I ducked my head down by the hole in the wall, said, "Who?" and covered it again with my boot. My voice instantly blasted through the cavern with a resounding "Whooooo!"

The lizard struggled and thrashed, trying to get away. "I must protect my egg."

"You!" Imishi exclaimed. "*You* stole Kukulkan's egg? You are nothing more than a common huchu lizard."

"You do not understand; I *am* Kukulkan," the lizard objected.

"Thief, thief!" Monty repeated with conviction.

I sensed a sort of desperation from the huchu lizard.

"You're an impostor," I said softly, "and you've done some very bad things."

The lizard stopped struggling. "I am the great . . . ," it began feebly.

I gave my head a firm shake and looked sternly into the miserable huchu lizard's eyes. "Don't make things worse. Why did you do it?"

"No one respected me, and I was lonely. I only wanted to show everyone that I am no different from Kukulkan. I needed the feathers to look like her. I would not have harmed the egg. I would have raised the child as my own, and it would have treated me as its mother." The voice became whiny. "I just needed a chance to show love. . . . I'm sorry."

I shook my head. "You stole a child—just to demonstrate how *great* you are and that you deserve love?" I could sense the huchu's desperate loneliness and misery, but that did not excuse what she had done. She was not an innocent. Kukulkan had been so distraught that she could well have killed us by mistake, thinking *we* had taken her egg.

"You're a liar, a thief, and a kidnapper. Those things do not make you *deserving*," I said firmly.

"I never meant to hurt anyone," the miserable lizard said.

I went back over to the stone nest, gently scooped up the egg, and placed it into the Guatemalan bag with my cacao pod. "You can't steal greatness or love—you have to earn it," I told the lizard after Monty and Imishi had let her go. "If you really want to be great, do something good for someone *else.* That will impress everyone a lot more than trying to be someone you're not."

We returned to Kir and Kukulkan to share the news. With the green orb shedding its light in the darkness of evening, Imishi and I told the strange story of the self-important huchu. I removed the cacao pod from my bag so that I could get a good grasp on the coppery egg and pull it out. The feathered serpent was ecstatic to see her egg. Accepting it from me, she tucked it tightly under one feathered wing and made a trilling, cooing sound. I started to put the pod back into my bag when Kukulkan noticed and touched the tip of her massive snout to the pod.

"Strong magic," she breathed warmly. "Healing magic." She bowed her head. "I am grateful."

I could feel waves of happiness rolling from

Kukulkan. She twirled in an excited spiral until she was almost completely upright. She then gradually lowered herself back onto the rocky volcanic mountainside in a smooth, even curl, like a neatly coiled rope with a mound of feathers on top. When she was settled, she opened the wing that cradled the coppery egg again to show us that it now shone with flecks of glitter, like the sparkles on the shell of my pod.

"Healthy," the feathered serpent said. "My egg will hatch soon." With that, she tucked the egg into the center of the feather-covered coil and settled down with a contented snaky sigh. "You sssssleep," she told us all in a soft voice. "I will guard you."

And sleep we did—all of us, right there on the side of the mountain. I still had that weird being-watched feeling, but I figured that Kukulkan could protect us from just about anything.

Monty perched protectively on the mound of Kukulkan's feathers, softly squawking, "Safe now, safe now." Kukulkan did not object, and Monty put his head under his wing.

It was not the most comfortable night we ever spent, but we were exhausted and easily fell asleep despite the rocky ground beneath us.

We awoke at dawn, sore and yet refreshed. I hate to admit it, but getting up early *felt* right. There was an urgency in my heart, pushing me to get to Kib Valley as soon as possible. I could sense the same need to get moving from Imishi and Kir.

While we slept, the lizard had come out of the cave and apologetically presented herself to the real Kukulkan, who had listened and forgiven her. I wondered if I had been too hard on the miserable creature.

After eating the last of our fairy food and breaking open the last pod of fairy water, sharing it amongst the group, I pointed to the lizard. "We can take her with us, if you need us to," I said to Kukulkan.

"No," she said. "I will keep the small Kuku with me. She will not be lonely."

It surprised me that the feathered serpent could be so forgiving after all the worry the smaller reptile had put her through. But legend said that Kukulkan was the wisest of creatures, so I trusted that she knew what was best. We said our good-byes to Kukulkan, who, after thanking us again, held her egg under one wing, tucked the huchu lizard under the other, and flew gently away using her two pairs of free wings.

We spent the morning walking around the slope of the volcano to the other side. As we traveled, we heard an occasional rumbling or felt a tremor from deep within the volcano, definitely not comforting. I still had that faint prickly feeling that someone—or some*thing*—was watching us. Finally we reached the point where we could begin our descent.

"I know where we are now!" Imishi said, excitement lighting her voice. "I can see the edge of the valley!"

Kir, thinking of his sire, trotted forward.

We carefully began our downward climb. White billows of steam and gray smoke rose from the tip of the cone far above us, making us all uneasy and eager to be away from the restless mountain. As we zigzagged on the steepest parts, we heard a crack and a boom. More clouds of steam puffed from the top of the mountain. The air was oppressively hot. Soon, little bits of something soft and warm began falling on us. Thinking that it was rain, I put a hand out to catch some drops, but instead of water, flecks of warm ash fell on my palm.

This could not be a good sign. My hand clenched, and my knees felt wobbly.

Kir gave a warning whinny.

Imishi pointed ahead to a flat drop-off directly below us. "We need to avoid that area," she said. "Those are the cliffs where the spider lives."

I consulted the map. "It looks like we can go either this direction or that." I pointed out the slopes to either side of the cliffs. "Once we get to the bottom, it's not far to the edge of the valley."

We began angling off to the right-hand side of the cliffs. There was a boom, like someone had fired off a cannon. Kir gave a wild whinny and backed up a few steps. With a whiz-*pow,* a large boulder landed where we had been standing a moment earlier. *BAM!* Another boulder landed in front of it. A crack appeared just above us, and a rivulet of red spurted out and began to run down toward us.

Lava!

"Wrong way, wrong way!" Monty squawked.

Kir wheeled and carried us with all the speed that caution allowed toward the far side of the cliffs. Small rocks tumbled down the slope toward us. Kir's hooves slipped a few times, but he managed to catch himself and keep going.

We had made it almost completely to the far side of the cliffs when another large boulder landed not far behind us. With a crack and rumble, the ground gave way beneath it, leaving a gaping hole open to the catacombs beneath. I shuddered. At least there was no lava coming toward us. There were still rocks flying through the air, however.

Imishi spread her wings to cover Monty, Kir, and me, protecting us from ash and small falling stones. When we were past the end of the cliffs, Kir headed further downslope, zigzagging again at the steep parts.

Imishi suddenly gasped and pointed to where the rock had broken open the catacombs. I looked. There, climbing out of the new jagged hole, was the ugliest and most terrifying creature I had ever seen or imagined.

A giant spider.

9

The Web

Imishi screamed.

My stomach did a somersault and then tried to crawl up into my throat. My mind scrambled to pull everything together that I had recently learned about dealing with creatures, especially innocents.

Kir paused. Behind me, Imishi put her head against my back and scrunched down low, as if trying to make herself as small and invisible as possible.

"That is the one—the spider that attacked me," Imishi said. "I know it."

I wondered if this spider could have been watching us, following us.

Monty muttered, "Not safe, not safe!"

Taking a deep breath, I sent my mind outward, carrying the thought *If you leave us alone, we'll leave you alone.*

The creature stopped on the slope just above us, slowly raising and lowering itself on its giant hairy legs, as if it was doing some sort of creepy spider push-ups.

Peace, calm, I sent to it, while all the hair on my arms prickled. *We don't want to hurt you; don't hurt us.*

The spider stopped moving. I thought I was finally getting somewhere when *bam!* The spider slammed my mind away like a baseball player hitting a home run—and it *hurt*!

"That is one rude spider," I said. And it was *not* an innocent.

The spider, balancing itself on four legs, swung its body back and made a trumpeting bellow that sounded like a bull elephant with a bit of rattlesnake thrown in. While it was still on its back four legs, something shot out from underneath it, straight at us—a strand of spider silk. Now, this wasn't transparent, wispy—almost pretty—spider silk like you might see in a garden or the corner of your attic. It was a sticky, ropy, mucus yellow strand as fat as my thumb.

Kir turned to protect us by heading back downhill, but it was too late. The spider rope tangled in his tail and stuck there. Monty fluttered unsteadily into the air, squawking in defiance at the giant spider, as

Imishi and I leapt off Kir's back and tried to help.

Imishi pulled her shell knife from the small sheath at her waist, but the spider was already reeling in the sticky rope, pulling Kir gradually back up the slope by his flaxen tail. The palomino was frantic. Imishi and I scrambled toward him but kept losing our footing on the slope. We were getting scraped and bruised, though at the time I hardly noticed. All I could think of was Kir.

Abruptly Kir put his feet solidly under him; then he backed up a few steps so the spider silk went a bit slack. Next he turned and galloped upslope. Avoiding the sticky rope, he charged straight at the spider. It reacted unlike any spider I had ever seen. (Then again, normal spiders don't usually fight horses.)

The spider set two more legs on the ground and reached out as if to do battle with the approaching horse. The arachnid's body was half again as big as Kir's, although the golden horse probably weighed more. The spider's legs were also longer than Kir's. Imishi and I could only watch as the eight-legged monster reached for our friend.

Monty fluttered above the spider, distracting it briefly while Kir ran past the spider toward its rear legs, turned, and kicked it full force right in its ugly spider butt. The spider flew through the air, releasing its sticky rope in its shock as it turned end over end and landed on its back with a squishy *thump,* halfway across the cliff top. Its legs were drawn in toward its stomach, and they wriggled as the spider tried to recover from the stunning blow and get itself upright again.

Imishi and I resumed our upward climb, unable to keep ourselves from glancing back. Monty landed on Kir's blanket and clung for dear life as the horse came to meet us, trailing the gluey rope from his tail. It seemed to catch on every rock.

"Try not to touch it," Imishi warned me. I cautiously wrapped my hands around Kir's tail, holding the spider rope up while Imishi cut through it with her shell knife.

Perched on the fairy-silk blanket, Monty supervised our work. "Time to go, time to go!"

We all knew this, of course; it wouldn't be long before the spider recovered and came after us. During our struggle we had worked our way back onto the steepest part of the trail. The cliffs beneath us were riddled with the spider's tunnels and caves, and crags of rock thrust up from below.

Looking down at that long drop and the sharp

rocks I could hit along the way made me feel dizzy. Keeping a grasp on my bag, I turned away from the cliffside to join Imishi and Kir on the downward trail again. The entire volcano seemed to rumble. The rocky ground beneath my feet disintegrated. I flailed my arms, frantically trying to grab at something, *anything.*

I felt myself falling into open air, head over heels.

Falling, falling . . .

My plunge came to a jarring stop that almost wrenched my arms out of their sockets. I felt myself going downward again; then I bounced upward a bit, fell down again, sprang up, fell down. . . . It was like hanging from a rubber band, and it happened again and again before I jolted to a stop.

I was hanging with my legs dangling over nothing. I looked up and saw that my hands were wrapped around and stuck to the strand of spiderweb that we had just cut away from Kir's tail. I had managed to grab it, and now it was glued fast to my hands.

Fifty feet above me, at the top of the cliff, Imishi's stricken face was staring down at me. All the color was gone from her cheeks, and I wondered if she was about to faint. Her face disappeared.

I looked around me for some way to get out of this mess. Six feet away on the cliff wall was a cave opening. If I could swing over there and get my feet under me, I might be able to cut the strand with a sharp rock.

I could sense from Kir that he, Monty, and Imishi were trying to figure out how to reach me. Through Kir's mind I could hear Imishi say that a fairy-silk rope would not solve the problem, since there was no way I could climb up it with my hands tied. Nor could they pull me up by the spider rope without risking getting caught in it themselves.

I heard Monty squawk, "Help, help! We're here, we're here!"

"The Kib Fairies will help us," Imishi agreed, "but with a broken wing I cannot get to the valley. And I cannot leave Zally. Kir, will you take Monty to deliver the message? Ask them to come help Imishi."

"Help Imishi, help Imishi," Monty repeated.

Kir neighed, shaking his flaxen mane. The parrot clung to the fairy-silk blanket while the palomino went down the steep slope.

I couldn't wait. Kicking back with my legs, then forward, then back again, then forward again, I started to swing myself toward the cave ledge. On the far side on top of the cliff, I saw the spider clinging to the cliff edge, *watching.* Then it clambered back into the hole it had come out of.

Above me, I saw Imishi's face again, followed by a loop of silky ribbon descending toward me. Maybe she was trying to lasso my feet so my friends could pull me back to the top of the cliff, just as they had dragged the tree trunk over to the jaguar's pit in the jungle. I could already see that the loop would be too far away to reach me, so I continued to swing. Finally I managed to touch the cave ledge with one foot, but I couldn't hold on.

I swung away again. I knew with part of my mind that my arms, shoulders, and neck hurt worse than they had ever hurt before in my life, but I couldn't focus on the pain or I would never escape. All I could concentrate on was the swinging, just like on a swing set. I pulled my legs back as far as they could go on my outward arc, then swung forward with all my might, pointing my toes toward the cave entrance.

The spider rope slipped. I plunged downward ten feet before springing to a stop again. I screamed. My forward momentum hadn't stopped yet, and I smacked feetfirst into the cliff wall. The jolt traveled from my feet up my legs. It drove every ounce of air out of my lungs, and I crumpled as my swing pulled me back. All my muscles went limp, and I just dangled there.

The spider rope slipped again—only a few feet

this time, but I realized that all my swinging back and forth must have loosened it from wherever it had stuck to the cliff above me. The rope swung me back toward the cliff wall again. I closed my eyes and held my breath.

Suddenly Imishi was there beside me. I felt her arms wrap around my waist and pull. My head seemed to spin, and for several dizzy moments I couldn't tell up from down. Then we landed on flat, cool rock. I opened my eyes to see that Imishi and I now sat in the cave opening toward which I had been swinging.

Confused, I gasped, "But I slipped! How . . ."

Imishi pulled out her shell knife and began to cut the spider rope from my hands. In a matter-of-fact voice she said, "I saw that you were going to fall, so I did the only thing I could: I flew."

"But you can't! Queen Patchouli said your wing would break if you tried to . . ." My voice trailed off as I noticed what I should have seen immediately.

Although Imishi's wings were spread proudly behind her, the one that had been broken and splinted was cracked, and the top half was folded down, dangling uselessly behind her.

I gasped again. "You didn't!"

"You are more important than my wing, Zally.

So is Queen Carmina. So are all of the innocents waiting for *our* help." At her words, tears welled up in my eyes.

Just then, from the tunnels deep within the cave behind us, came the same trumpeting bellow we had heard earlier. My friend and I quickly got to our feet to face our attacker. This was the last thing in the world Imishi wanted to face—and my *own* worst nightmare—so I was proud of the way she stood beside me. She had my back, and I had hers. Actually, we both pressed our backs to the cave wall at the side of the entrance.

Imishi brandished her small shell knife, and I prepared my mind to push away the beast. I held up my hands, which were now free, and clenched them into fists, although I wasn't sure what I could do against Spiderzilla with my bare hands. Still, we planted our feet and prepared for the attack.

Rays of sunlight slanted in through the cave opening.

And there it was: the spider.

I tried to calm it again. As before, it bounced up and down on all eight legs and threw my thoughts back in my face. It stepped closer and balanced on its four back legs. Then it raised the front half of its body and trumpeted again. This time, the trumpet was answered by a deep, growling roar.

Then everything happened in a blur.

There was a flurry of hairy spider legs and tawny gold with black spots. The spider flew up and hit the ceiling. Fur, claws, and spider legs flashed. With a bellow, the stunned spider shot past us out of the cave. It hung motionless for a split second in midair, then fell. A moment later, we heard a *thud* as it hit the rocks below.

In the center of the cavern, with one spider leg still grasped in her jaws, stood the jaguar whom we had freed from the pit in the jungle. Her jade eyes glowed, and the thoughts that came from the cat were fierce and protective. All of a sudden I understood that for the past day, every time I thought we were being watched or followed, we *were*. It had been the jaguar—not stalking us, but keeping watch over us.

The jungle cat padded to the ledge at the cave entrance. She dropped the spider leg over the edge, then, with a swift turn, butted her head against Imishi's shoulder. She gave a soft growl and nudged the fairy toward the other side of the cave entrance. Though I felt no danger to myself from the jaguar, this alarmed me—until I heard Imishi gasp.

"Thank you!" Imishi knelt in the shadows for a minute, picking something up, and brought it back to show me.

She held out a cluster of delicate indigo flowers. "Shadeblossom," she said. "Will you keep it in your bag for me? I want to give it to Queen Carmina."

I tucked the flowers into my bag, and the jaguar rubbed her body against me. I patted her tawny back and pressed my cheek against her fur.

"Thank you," I whispered. "I was afraid of you, you know. I still am, but I'm glad we met. You showed me how important it is to trust the map in my heart."

Imishi put a hand on the huge cat's back. "I judged you without knowing you, and for that I am sorry. You are a true friend."

The rumbling reply that came from the jaguar's throat sounded just like a purr.

At that moment, a commotion of flapping wings came from outside, and we all heard a familiar voice. "We're here, we're here!"

10

The Kib Valley

Kib Valley wasn't anything like I had imagined. The fairies from Imishi's tribe who rescued us put us into a woven sling like a hammock. Like Imishi, the fairies all wore dresses patterned like animals or birds. Although we had left the jaguar behind in the cave, I got the impression that as long as I remained in Aventurine, she would never be far away.

After the fairies set off for Kib Valley, Imishi's first questions were about the fairy queen and the king of the horses, Kir's father. The news from our fairy rescuers was not good.

From the hammock, I got an amazing view of the valley. To keep Imishi's mind occupied, I asked her questions about everything I was seeing. My first impression of Kib was *green*—as far as the valley reached. It was the kind of lush, exuberant green I recognized from pictures of places like Hawaii, Belize, and Guatemala.

The valley floor was a broad bowl that Imishi told me had been an inland sea thousands of years ago. Over the ages, the sea had dried up, and eruptions and earthquakes had filled the valley with rich volcanic soil. The dirt and rocks of the valley were black. The far valley wall was flat, with strands of color sweeping through it. When the sunlight hit it, the entire wall sparkled, as if it were set with millions of tiny gems. Imishi explained that the rock wall had sheared away in an ancient earthquake to reveal the fossils and shells of creatures that had once inhabited the inland sea. Those shells were what glittered in the rock wall.

Imishi gave me an anxious look. "Breathe."

I realized I had been holding my breath, and I let it out in a smile and a sigh. I hadn't noticed the buildings at first, but now I did. They reminded me of photos I had seen of the city of Tikal in Guatemala. A newer image appeared in my mind as well: the layout of the fairy city was identical to the map of ruined Ool-Kib on the observatory wall in the jaguar's jungle!

Below us were Mayan-style pyramids, flat courtyards, a spectacular spiral amphitheater that reminded me of a nautilus shell, pools and fountains, tiers of hanging gardens, and an observatory. On the hillsides, terraces of planted crops were dotted with ornate storage buildings. All of these things were made from a combination of stone, shell, and living plants that blended together in a magnificent mosaic on a background of green. It all looked so . . . natural.

"We're almost there." Imishi pointed below us.

Coming down the slope into the valley was Kir with Monty on his back. From far up the valley in the other direction, a herd of golden horses galloped toward the buildings at the center, where their sick king waited. The fairies carrying us started flying downward in a spiral to meet Kir and Monty. It wasn't until we were almost on the ground that we could really see the effects of the fairy queen's blindness on the valley.

Harried fairies fluttered from one building to another, their arms laden with trays of food, buckets of water, bandages, blankets, straw, and so on. By the time we arrived beside Kir at the first cluster of buildings, I could see the signs of neglect. Fallen leaves cluttered courtyards and fountains. Sick or hurt animals were crowded into stalls, pens, chambers, and sheds along the outside of the buildings. Imishi pointed to a broad swath of terrace gardens alongside a long building.

"This is the medicinal herb garden," she said. It was tangled and overgrown with weeds. "It seems nobody has tended it since I left," she added quietly.

Monty gave a questioning squawk. "We're here, we're here?"

"We're definitely here," I agreed, "and there seems to be plenty of work to do. I just have no idea where to start."

"We start with the queen," Imishi said in a firm voice. "If we can help her, that will help more innocents than anything else we could do."

I sensed Kir's impatience to see his sire, though, and make sure that he was receiving proper care. I tried to comfort him with soothing thoughts.

Something came out of the long building and bounded toward us like a gigantic one-legged rabbit.

"Grimblehart!" Imishi cried, brightening.

When the hopping thing was almost next to us, I realized it was not an animal, but a person—a person about twice as tall as I, with only one leg. He had a huge head, with a fringe of fluffy black hair, a blobby nose, wide gray eyes that blinked constantly, and a toothy smile.

"It's okay," Imishi assured me in a whisper. "He's the nicest one-legged ogre you could ever hope to meet." When Grimblehart stopped, she launched herself into his arms for a fierce hug and said, "I've been so worried."

"Dear Imishi," Grimblehart said, gingerly patting her back and trying to not further injure her broken wing. "There's plenty to be worried about, there is. Creatures dying, nobody knowing exactly what to do, all of us working night and day, and nothing gettin' no better. The valley's in a sorry state, missy, enough to make a grown ogre cry."

"Will you take us to Queen Carmina?" my friend asked.

"We can try," Grimblehart said, "but I'm afraid she won't see nobody—meaning no disrespect to Her Majesty's blindness. She says she's lost her gift and don't want no one to see her like that. Hardly eats, poor thing." He heaved a blustery sigh and motioned for us to follow him. Monty hopped onto Imishi's shoulder, and Kir clopped behind us.

We passed through two infirmaries. It hurt to see all of these animals and magic creatures who needed help beyond what the fairies caring for them could give. Tears prickled behind my eyelids. What if—what if I *failed* in my quest? What if I had come all this way with Imishi and this was a test I couldn't pass? I wasn't a doctor or a veterinarian. What could I do to truly help?

We stopped to look into a room where a once-magnificent stallion lay near death. "King Xel himself,"

Grimblehart murmured. Monty remained abnormally quiet.

My throat tightened, and I could feel myself starting to panic. I couldn't be responsible for all of this, could I?

Kir gave me a hard nudge from behind, followed by a loud snort.

Imishi must have seen the look of uncertainty on my face. She took my hand. "My cousin is right. You have to do it. This is why you came."

Noble horse faces appeared at the window, looking expectantly. Imishi murmured to Kir as I went over to King Xel. I knelt and laid a hand on his head, trying to pick up his thoughts. A swirl of fever dreams told me that the king of horses was gravely ill. I had no idea what to do.

I stood to give Kir a hug, squelching my feelings of self-doubt and inadequacy. Kir was counting on me. Imishi was counting on me. These horses were family. *Everyone* was counting on me. And when everyone is counting on you, it's selfish to wimp out.

"Okay," I said to Grimblehart, straightening my shoulders. "Take us to Queen Carmina."

Kir stayed behind with his sire while the ogre led Imishi and me to the palace of the fairy queen. The palace was a tall step pyramid of polished gray stone.

From the outside, the building looked like it was about a half mile high. Up the sides of the pyramid ran hundreds of shallow steps. Hopping, the ogre led us straight up the center of the palace pyramid. Imishi kept her good wing and her broken one folded together and tucked up behind her. Monty took his position on her shoulder.

I tried to count the stairs as we climbed, but I lost track after about two hundred. Already weary from our journey, we were completely winded by the time we reached the uppermost level, to which Queen Carmina had withdrawn.

The queen's chambers were airy and brightly sunlit from slits and holes expertly carved in the stone block walls. I didn't even see the queen at first. Half hidden in a shadowy corner of the room, she was curled on her throne with her arms wrapped around her legs. She had on a shapeless brown garment, and her wings were tucked back.

Imishi ran forward, and taking one of the queen's hands, she knelt at her side.

"I have no wish for visitors," Queen Carmina murmured. Her voice sounded as if it came from miles away.

"It's all right," Imishi said. "Prince Kir and I found help."

I moved forward and saw that the queen's expression was bleak. "There is no help. I have lost my gift," she said.

Monty gave another uncertain squawk. "We're here, we're here?"

Imishi shot me a look. "It can't be true, can it? Is her illness hopeless?"

I swallowed hard. "I don't know. Give me a moment." I closed my eyes and let my mind wander, just as I had when making the Aventurine map.

Thoughts rose. Queen Patchouli had sent me here, hadn't she? She had said the Inocentes Lineage was the best choice for this quest. She believed in me. I would have to observe, listen, and gather facts until I figured out what I *could* do.

"Tell me everything," I said to the queen. Then I realized I couldn't do it alone. "Tell *us* everything," I added, smiling at Imishi. She smiled back and nodded.

Grimblehart picked up a couple of stools from the edge of the room. He set out one each for Imishi and me, next to Queen Carmina's throne. We sat. Imishi introduced me to the queen and explained how I had volunteered to help her and Kir. "Zally risked her life to bring us back here to help you."

Embarrassed, I quickly changed the subject. "Have there been any changes in your eyesight since

Imishi left?" I asked, hoping to draw Queen Carmina out. Staring straight ahead with her blind mother-of-pearl eyes, the fairy queen shook her head but said nothing. How could I learn enough about the queen to help her if she just sat in her chair in miserable silence? Maybe she couldn't tell us everything.

It was Imishi who made the first crack in her queen's shell with a question. "Would you like to hear about Kir's and my journey to the Willowood, and about our adventures on the way back with Zally?"

The queen sat up straighter on her throne and gave a tiny nod—the most interest she had shown so far. For the next hour Imishi and I described all that had happened to us. Imishi reported on our marsh adventure, and I joined in to narrate the attack of the marsh troll. I could see the queen was drawn into our story. Finally she began to ask questions.

As we talked to Queen Carmina, Grimblehart hopped back and forth. He set a small table for us and spread it with shell plates of fairy delicacies: tidbits of cheese, sliced fruits, a bowl of nuts, a chunk of honeycomb, and shell cups filled with liquid. Now that the queen was wrapped up in our tales of adventure, Grimblehart saw his chance and pressed a cup filled with a purple juice into her hand.

She drank without noticing what she was doing

and urged Imishi and me to continue. The ogre exchanged the cup for a plate of fruits and cheeses, from which Queen Carmina began to nibble. Grimblehart gave Imishi and me a wink and a broad grin. Some of the tension inside me began to relax, and I had a kind of revelation as the pieces of the journey blended together in my mind.

Because you're reading all of this, maybe it was obvious to you, but it took me that long to really understand my quest. It wasn't about passing tests or guiding people or impressing anyone with how smart I was and teaching them not to underestimate me. The quest wasn't about waving a wand and making cool things happen. It wasn't even about being able to talk to animals, although that was a part of the bigger picture.

My quest was about learning to listen to what a person or a creature needed, and being willing to do whatever I could—just like my mother and Abuelita did. They took the time to listen, to understand. Certainly Mamá and Abuelita had done that for me, offering hugs, a cup of *chocolatl,* and a friendly ear. Other things began to fall into place, like the fact that Abuelita had given me the cacao pod as a symbol of our lineage, as well as of our magic and our heritage. I loved to help people and animals and had been doing it most of my life already! The Inocentes gift infused the whole Guevara family now. We not only fed people through our bakery, we reached out to offer other help. Feeding their souls . . .

The cacao pod! I sat up straight. Imishi was describing our hasty exit from the swamps when I excused myself for a moment and whispered my request in the ogre's ear. With a grin, he hopped in front of me and led me to the palace kitchen.

I pulled the cacao pod out of my satchel, along with Abuelita's recipe for *chocolatl* that Queen Patchouli had given me. I quickly scanned the recipe, then looked around the kitchen.

Surprisingly, they had everything that I needed.

Aventurine Chocolatl

1 Kib chili pepper, split lengthwise
(seeds removed using gloves)

2 cups water

30 magic cacao beans

2 tablespoons fine cornmeal

4 cups light cream

1 large vanilla bean, split lengthwise

1 pinch salt

2 sticks Aventurine cinnamon

2 tablespoons honey

With Grimblehart's help, I found a medium pot and very carefully cut the chili pepper lengthwise. I put on gloves to remove all the seeds, knowing that if I used my bare hands and then later touched my eyes, it would really hurt. Then I boiled the chili pepper with two cups of water until the liquid was reduced to one cup. With a spoon, I carefully strained the chili pepper from the water and set the chili water aside. While the chili water was boiling, I took all of the cacao beans from the pod, toasted them in a flat pan, and let them cool. In another flat pan, I quickly toasted the fine cornmeal and set it aside to cool as well.

In a large pot, I cooked the cream, vanilla bean, salt, and Aventurine cinnamon sticks over medium heat, stirring constantly until bubbles appeared around the edge. The Aventurine cinnamon sticks were flecked with copper and made the mixture glow orange until I reduced the heat to low. Then I added the honey and whisked the mixture until the honey dissolved. I took the pot off the heat and removed the vanilla bean and cinnamon sticks.

When the cocoa beans were cool, I ground them to a powder using a *molcajete* and put the ground cacao into a medium bowl with the toasted fine cornmeal.

While I worked, I thought about the fairy queen

and how much she was needed. I considered how brave it had been for Kir and Imishi to leave in search of help. How lucky I had been that Queen Patchouli had sent me here. I had seen so much of Aventurine and made some very good friends. As these thoughts ran through my head, the ground cacao began to glitter with sparkles of gold. *Is this the magic of the cacao?* I wondered.

A quarter cup at a time, I stirred two cups of the cream mixture into the cacao-cornmeal bowl and kept stirring until the thick liquid was smooth. After pouring this mixture from the bowl back into the pot with the remaining cream mixture, I returned the pot to low heat to simmer. Then, a bit at a time, I poured in the chili-infused water, tasting it until the flavor was spicy, but not too strong. Lastly, I whisked the whole mixture until it was frothy. Finished, I took the *chocolatl* pot off the heat and poured the drink into four heavy mugs on a tray that Grimblehart brought me. The cacao pod itself had closed once more, and I put it back in my bag. I had never been so thankful for the long hours I'd spent in the kitchen of my family's bakery.

Grimblehart hopped beside me as I carried the

tray of steaming cups of *chocolatl* back to the queen's chambers. The smells of cacao, chili, vanilla, and cinnamon filled the air. Still engrossed in Imishi's story, the queen readily accepted a cup of the warm, fragrant liquid from me. I gave one cup to the ogre, handed one to Imishi, and kept one for myself, setting the tray off to the side.

11

The Healing

When all of us were seated, Imishi and I finished telling the story about the volcano, the spider, and the jaguar. I took the Shadeblossom from my pouch and gave it to my friend, who presented it to the fairy queen. Queen Carmina gasped in amazement. This gave me the opening I needed to ask questions about how the queen had been blinded and whether she knew of any cure.

The queen gave a sigh. "I am afraid there could be no cure for this blindness, even if I still had my healing powers."

"Can you tell me more about what your powers were like—how they worked?" I asked encouragingly. I didn't quite understand this yet, and it seemed like the powers might be the key to everything.

A wistful look came over Queen Carmina's face.

"I had the gift of identification, of diagnosis. Simply by looking at any creature, I could tell what was wrong. Once I understood and told my fairies what the problem was, it was a simple matter to direct them in what to do for the healing poultices. That part is not magic, but observation. And how can I observe without my eyesight?"

Imishi noted, "We have all the splints and poultices, bandages, and healing drafts, but without the queen to tell us which illness to treat, we are lost."

There was a nagging something that didn't quite make sense to me. "So your gift, or magic, or whatever that was—you just looked straight at a person or creature, and anything that was wrong would pop into your head?"

Carmina seemed taken aback; then she said, "No, not exactly. By looking, I could see a creature limp, or an ogre's hair falling out, or perspiration running down a pale face, or a rash on the legs. Things like that. Then by touching them, I could feel a fever, a tremor in the muscles, and so on. By listening, I could hear a cough. A certain smell could warn me of a specific illness. All of those things I was able to put together in a way I simply cannot explain. And then, yes, I would simply *know* what was wrong."

Tears filled Imishi's eyes. "I am so sorry, my

queen. It is my fault that you lost your sight and your gift. I had hoped that the Shadeblossom—"

The queen squeezed Imishi's hand and shook her head. "I know of someone else it can help, though."

"All right," I said. "I understand that you were blinded by the spider poison. That's how you lost your eyesight. But how exactly did you lose your *gift*?"

Queen Carmina shrugged as though this were obvious. "I lost my sight. I can no longer see the patients who come to me for help. Without my vision, I am powerless."

"But the poison didn't actually change your magic or make it go away, did it?" I pressed.

"Does it matter?" The queen hung her head. "I need all of my senses to understand what is wrong."

"But Imishi can see," I pointed out. "All of your other fairies can see, can't they?"

"We do not know what to look for," Imishi said. "We cannot interpret signs of illness or injury that Her Majesty would instantly recognize."

We all sipped our *chocolatl*. The flavors of cacao and spices mingled with a hint of sweetness on our tongues. The queen held her cup close to her face and breathed in the comforting scents with pleasure.

While we sat in silence, I thought for a moment. "You still have your mind, your hearing, your taste, your senses of smell and touch, right?" I asked.

"Yes, but . . ." The queen's voice trailed off.

"Then what if someone *told* you that their leg hurt, or that they were limping? Instead of looking at it—searching for a bulge or lump—couldn't you examine it with your fingers?"

The queen cocked her head to one side. "Perhaps. But that is not enough. I need to know so much more."

"Then ask," I said. "Guide us. Tell me something you might need to know. Pretend Grimblehart is the patient."

The ogre grinned. "I'd be happy to be the patient, if it will help Her Majesty."

Queen Carmina nodded gratefully and asked her first question. "What color is Grimblehart's skin?"

"A pale, blotchy grayish green," I answered immediately. "Except for his knuckles—they're very red."

The queen reached over to touch the ogre's hand and ran her fingers along his knuckles. She nodded. A small smile crept onto her face. "Then my friend is quite healthy," she concluded, "though perhaps he has been washing too many dishes." Now her smile grew so that her dimples showed for the first time. "But I have an ointment that's good for that."

"See?" I said. "You can still do lots of good, Queen Carmina."

Imishi's face lit up at the sight of the queen smiling. "I will be your eyes, Majesty. I can look at the sick and wounded for you and describe everything."

The queen squeezed Imishi's hand. "It could work. And with practice, I can teach you what to look for. But I must help you and our faithful parrot friend first."

"No," Imishi said gently but firmly. "Our lives are not in danger. We must find those who are in greatest need."

"Then I will rely on you to tell me which creatures those are," Queen Carmina said. She stood, took a deep breath, and spread her wings, which were a vibrant ruby red.

Monty hopped impatiently from one foot to the other and squawked, "Get to work, get to work!"

The *chocolatl* made from the beans of my cacao pod seemed to have an extra special restorative property, because even after we climbed down the hundreds of steps, Imishi and me each holding one of the queen's hands, none of us were tired. In fact, we all felt energized and eager to get started.

Queen Carmina, Imishi, and I spent the remainder of the afternoon visiting countless cubicles, stalls, mangers, ponds, nests, nooks, and crannies where sick or injured innocents had been staying for the last few weeks in Kib Valley. First we went to see Kir's sire, Xel, the king of horses. Xel lay in a corner on a bed of straw. A bowl of alfalfa and oats nearby seemed not to have been touched.

When I felt the waves of anxiety and heartsickness radiating from Kir, I threw my arms around the golden horse's neck and buried my face in his mane. "We'll do everything in our power to help," I promised.

Kir nickered and bobbed his head. From the window, the faces of the other horses in the herd looked in with concern.

Imishi led the queen over to Xel, and the fairy healer knelt beside the horse to examine him. "I am sorry it took me so long to visit you, cousin," Queen Carmina said. To Imishi, she added, "He feels warm, and he is too weak to stand. How does he look?"

Imishi cleared her throat. "Tired. He doesn't seem to be able to hold his head up very high. He's wheezing a lot, and there is a sticky substance coming from his eyes." After that, the fairy girl appeared to be at a loss for words.

"How are his hooves?" Queen Carmina prodded. "Does he have any wounds?"

Again, Imishi described what she saw.

I felt a nudge from behind and took a few steps toward the sick horse. Another nudge, and I was standing by Imishi. Behind me, Kir gave a whinny. I understood what he meant for me to do. What had I been thinking? I sat down cross-legged near Xel's head. I looked into his sickly eyes and started thinking comforting thoughts, as I had with Kir.

We're here now; we'll help you. We're friends. The queen is a good healer. Then I opened my mind to allow him to think back at me. After Imishi finished her description, I said to the queen, "Xel is having trouble catching a deep breath, and it hurts when he breathes."

The queen raised a hand, as if looking for something. Two of the fairies who had followed us into the room came forward to offer their help. Queen Carmina quickly described a root and herbs and asked the fairies to boil and mix them with oats for the ailing horse. She also told the fairies to apply a special ointment to Xel's eyes and boil a pot of herbs in the corner of the room so that the king of horses might breathe

the healing vapor. When those two fairies had flitted off, two more fairies appeared.

Last, the fairy queen held out the Shadeblossom that Imishi and I had brought her and told King Xel to eat it. "This will begin your healing immediately and make the herbs more powerful. You should feel stronger within the hour."

Kir took heart when Queen Carmina assured him that the king of horses would be completely healed within a week. We left the herd and Kir behind to watch over his sire.

In the next chamber, a long-legged bird was covered with a blue growth. The two fairies following us were assigned to his care.

As we moved from chamber to chamber, we developed a routine. The fairy queen did an examination by touch, smell, and hearing. Imishi gave descriptions of how the creature looked on the outside and anything unusual that she could see. Queen Carmina asked questions of each patient, and I gleaned what useful information I could from the minds of those who could not speak. After each diagnosis, a pair of fairies carried out the queen's instructions, and a new pair arrived.

After a while, Grimblehart sent us outside to a

courtyard with a deep pool, where we met a mermaid who could hardly swim. By the time darkness fell, every fairy of the Kib tribe had already been assigned at least three patients and was returning for another assignment. All of the seriously ill patients were taken care of and being treated.

At this point, for the sake of speed, every creature who could walk, fly, crawl, slither, or hop was gathered in front of the palace pyramid, instead of the queen going from place to place. Grimblehart brought her fresh clothing—a flowing dress in a kaleidoscope of animal patterns. Several fairies from the tribe brought braziers and torches and set them up at the base of the palace pyramid, where we continued our work.

Finally, Monty. Queen Carmina had one of her fairies make a special brew that she said would help him regrow his tail feathers in a matter of weeks. Carmina prescribed a slightly different brew for Imishi and reset her broken wing. "No flying for at least three hours," the fairy queen warned my friend.

Imishi laughed out loud and clapped her hands with delight.

Suddenly the night sky overhead was filled with hundreds of swirling lights and a whisper of voices.

"Are those swamp gnats?" I asked in alarm.

Imishi giggled. "No, those are fairy lights. Just wait."

The lights swirled downward. As they did, they grew larger, and I could see more than a hundred fairies, all carrying torches.

Monty squawked, "They're here, they're here!" as Queen Patchouli of the Willowood Fairies landed in front of us, holding a torch that sparkled with diamond-clear fire.

"We are indeed here—to help," Queen Patchouli said. "We brought fairies from six tribes. And we brought dinner."

The Willowood Fairies and the friends they had gathered set to work in a whirlwind of activity. Tables began arriving from every direction. The fairies set them up in concentric circles, along with seats for everyone who was there. The brightly colored fairy torches lit the circles. Next, platters of rosemary biscuits and jam made of red fruits like strawberries, raspberries, and some fruits I didn't recognize, which must be special to Aventurine, began arriving, along with pitchers of nectar. Without waiting to be asked, Imishi described the scene for Queen Carmina, whose face glowed with delight.

Before I knew it, we were all sitting down to eat

together and celebrate the healing of Kib Valley. No one could have been more surprised than I when Queen Patchouli herself stood, raised her goblet of nectar, and proposed a toast. "To Zally, for her courage, for bringing hope back to Kib Valley, and for showing us the way in these dark times."

I blushed furiously, and all of the fairies raised their goblets to drink. But I couldn't take all the credit. I stood and held my own goblet high. "And to Prince Kir and Imishi, who risked their lives by leaving Kib Valley to find help, and who helped me learn to use my gifts. Without them and Monty, I never could have made it here. They are true friends and true heroes." The fairies all drank to the toast, and I sat back down.

Now Queen Carmina lifted her voice and her goblet. "To Imishi, Prince Kir, Monty, and our fairy-godmother-in-training, Zally, for bringing healing to us all." Although the fairies drank to the toast and went back to talking with each other, I choked on a swallow of nectar.

Beside me, Imishi turned pale. "But we didn't heal *you,* Queen Carmina," she said.

Queen Carmina shook her head, beaming. "But you *have.* Zally helped me find my way out of the despair in which I had become lost. Imishi, you helped me understand that an injury, no matter how crippling it may seem, is not the end of my usefulness. And the two of you, along with Kir, have shown me that I am not alone. Every creature who we help is someone who may return the favor or help someone else in need." She lifted her goblet once more and said, "Thank you, all of you. You healed something far more important than my eyes. You have healed my heart."

As everyone cheered, Queen Patchouli leaned toward me. "Your quest was a success, Zally; you are on your way to becoming a fairy godmother."

"Oh! That reminds me," I said, pulling the map from my bag and handing it to her. "Here."

Queen Patchouli regarded it with a smile. "This map will be important in the training of many more fairy-godmothers-to-be." With that, she rang a glass bell that she seemed to produce out of thin air. Her fairies began flitting about, clearing everything as the banquet wound down.

While Queen Patchouli and Queen Carmina talked late into the night, Imishi, Kir, and I went for a walk. King Xel's fever was gone, and he had fallen into a restful sleep, so Kir no longer carried his worry; instead he gamboled like a foal. Imishi, her wing healed, fluttered into the air after every few steps. I wondered how my happiness showed.

A field of stars glittered overhead. For an hour, we took turns pointing out the animal constellations to each other. Then Imishi showed us her herb garden. Seeing all of the medicinal plants reminded me that Imishi had said Kib Valley had nothing like my cacao pod.

I pulled the talisman out of my bag and broke it open. I took out a few of the beans, knelt, and buried them in the earth of the herb garden. Kneeling beside me, Imishi covered the planting with both hands and closed her eyes. Looking over our shoulders, Kir made a gentle blowing sound, giving his blessing. The ground beneath Imishi's fingers sparkled as if sprinkled by, well, fairy dust.

She opened her eyes and nodded at me. By the time we stood up, wiping the dirt from our hands, my cacao pod had resealed once more, and a green shoot had sprung up from the ground. The three of us took a few steps back and watched. Within minutes, there was a full-grown tree with cacao pods of its own. In my hand, my cacao pod talisman glowed. The cacao pods on the new tree glowed in response.

Imishi gave me a hug. "Thank you for sharing

the healing power of this plant. Whenever I see it, I will think of you."

Kir whinnied, shoving his head against me once more, this time playfully. Imishi and I both threw our arms around his neck and hugged him.

When we returned from our walk, Queen Patchouli and Queen Carmina asked to meet with me. Two fairy queens! With me, Zally Guevara!

"What did you think of your quest?" Queen Patchouli asked, pouring me a goblet of nectar.

I took a drink. "It's the hardest thing I've done in my whole life, and I hope I never have to do anything that scary or dangerous again," I said truthfully. I drew a deep breath. "But I will if I have to."

"Thank you," Queen Carmina said with a catch in her voice.

"We're all grateful," Queen Patchouli agreed. "And what of your map, Zally? Would you do anything differently?"

I grinned. "The map is pretty amazing and wonderful, but it sure would have been useful if it showed places in three dimensions, so we could plan better for the terrain. And if I could wish for any improvement I wanted, I'd add a way to ask the map questions and have it answer them."

"Very well," Queen Patchouli said. "You have the ability to make that happen, Zally; it is part of your gift."

"Although you could change the map yourself," Queen Carmina said, "I think we can help you make it even better. Will you trust us to do that?"

"Of course," I said. "What do I need to do?"

"Touch both maps," Queen Patchouli said. I put one hand on each of the twinned maps. Queen Patchouli covered my right hand with hers and raised her left hand to the sky, palm up. Queen Carmina completed the semicircle with a hand on mine and one raised.

I felt as if I was falling into a mapping trance, but the feeling lasted only a moment. When I focused my eyes again, one of the maps was gone.

I bit my lip. I had worked so hard to make those maps! "What happened?" I asked.

Queen Carmina smiled. "You guided me out of my despair, showing me that the truest map is in the heart. Now the map of Aventurine is in your heart. And the intuition of your heart is in our map as well. You will always be linked to the Aventurine map, even in the waking world."

I was speechless.

"The other features you wished for are in the

map now," Queen Patchouli said. "Is there a greeting you would like to add?"

I thought for a moment. When I spoke, a spray of red-gold sparks rose to form glittering words in the air above the map. "It should say,

Sister dreamers,

This is the only map of Aventurine. I hope it helps you on your quest. Aventurine's geography can change for each dream or dreamer, so this map is not the kind of map you are used to.

Zally

When I finished my greeting, the words dissolved and fell into the map. I touched the spot where they had fallen, and an image of the volcano grew from the page and hovered in three dimensions above it, like a hologram. It was perfect.

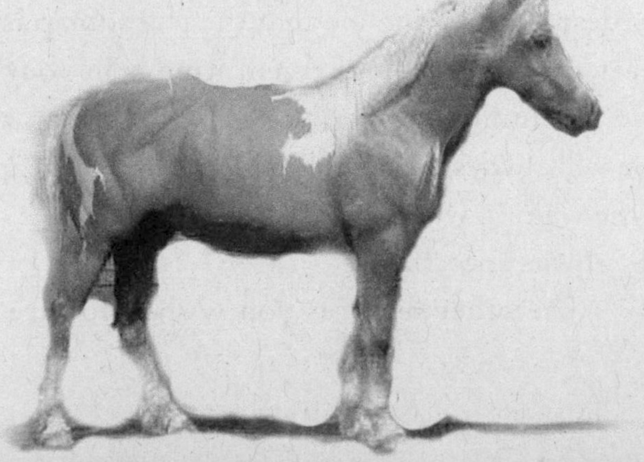

"Now *that*'s a helpful map," I said. "Is there anything else you wanted to talk about?"

Queen Patchouli shook her head. "It's time to say good-bye to your friends, Zally," she said. "For now, at least."

Then Kir, Imishi, and I went for a farewell ride, and the jaguar ran beside us in the moonlight.

12

The Magic

The morning light and a tickling on my nose woke me.

My eyes snapped open.

I was disoriented at first: there were no mountains; no valleys; no lush, dense jungles; no beautiful golden horses. No fairies. Just the walls of my room, close enough to touch. I was back in my sky bed, wearing the same outfit I'd had on before going to Aventurine.

The new mama cat was beside me in the bed. She must have jumped onto one of my shelves and from there onto my bed. How she had gotten there didn't matter as much as the fact that she was definitely in labor! She was curled up against something else in the bed—my woven bag.

I carefully pulled the cacao pod out. It was completely intact, with a sparkle and sheen to its hull.

I thought of all the adventures our family talisman must have had—with me, Mamá, Abuelita, and other fairy godmothers before us in the Inocentes Lineage. I smiled and petted the gray mama cat. "You are going to have some amazing kittens."

I carefully got out of the bed and returned with towels and an old waterproof baby-changing pad, which I carefully placed under the cat. In all, the labor took several hours and produced a litter of five kittens. I cleaned the kittens and my bed, during which I made a plan.

Entrusting the new family to Abuelita and J.J., I took a shower. After washing my hair—no longer in its vines—and braiding it into one thick plait that hung over my shoulder, I hurried downstairs to the bakery and set to work.

Sunday wasn't a normal workday, since the bakery was closed. In fact, our parents usually let us do more or less whatever we wanted on Sundays while they did prep work for the coming week. But since Mamá wouldn't be home from her trip to Guatemala until supper and Papá was still working on the quarterly taxes, I decided I didn't want them to worry about such things today—I was determined to take care of the shop myself.

I disinfected the inside of the pastry display case,

mopped the floors, and refilled the bins of flour, sugar, cinnamon, cocoa powder, chili powder, and nuts in the kitchen. For the first time in as long as I could remember, the work didn't bother me. These were things that needed to be done, just like my quest in Aventurine.

Mopping the floor reminded me of the marsh that Imishi, Kir, and I had slogged through. When I ran the last of the baking pans through the huge industrial dishwasher, the steam that billowed out reminded me of the dense, humid jungle. Scraping out the large ovens made me think of climbing the side of the volcano. In comparison to what I had done in Aventurine, any tasks in the bakery seemed almost insignificant. The work was easier now.

I hummed a tune and twirled with the mop, dancing with it. I knew it was silly, but I was actually enjoying myself a bit. I wasn't trying to be a Goody Two-shoes, and I wasn't trying to earn brownie points or pass any tests.

You want to know what I think? Here it is. Maybe that's one of the perks of being a fairy-godmother-in-training: some of the everyday stuff that you do to help people gets easier and more fun. It's not simple, like it is in *Cinderella* when the fairy godmother just waves a wand and makes a dress or turns a pumpkin into a coach. The magic isn't all flashy and dazzly like that. But there's something magical just the same.

Maybe that's why, when my brothers and Abuelita arrived two hours later, the work seemed to get finished in a heartbeat.

I spent the next hour drawing a map of New York, with J.J. sitting beside me in the living room. I managed to fit in plenty of the landmarks in Manhattan, drawing little cartoon figures for the Statue of Liberty, Broadway, the Metropolitan Museum of Art—and our own bakery.

At the top, I neatly printed ALMA DE CHOCOLATE along with our address, our phone number, and the hours our shop was open. I showed it to Papá and told him that I'd like to put it up in the shop window.

"That's wonderful, *mi'ja,*" he said. "But do you know what else I think we should do? If you don't mind, I'd like to make a whole stack of copies and give them out whenever a lost tourist comes into the shop. We can use it as an advertisement, too, leave some with the concierge at that hotel up the street. I can even have Antonio scan this and put it up on our Web site."

I blushed, surprised at his enthusiasm. "It's . . . just a map."

"It is exactly the map we need, *mi'ja,*" he said. "And it shows our bakery looking just as important in our city as it is in our hearts."

Our family dinner celebrating Mamá's return may not have been a fairy banquet, but it was close. Abuelita, my three brothers, and I all pitched in on the cooking, so that by the time Papá brought her home from the airport, dinner was ready.

Mamá told stories about her trip to Guatemala. There was lots of laughter when she described how a family of rabbits had tried to take up residence in the new schoolhouse that was under construction.

At one point during dinner, Mamá stopped talking and just stared at me for a minute, as if trying to figure something out. Then she gave me a small smile and a nod and continued talking. After dinner, I flitted back and forth between the table and the kitchen, clearing plates, all the while thinking about the beautiful fairies cleaning up after the banquet.

Everyone made a fuss over the mama cat and her new kittens, which now slept in a basket in a corner of the living room. J.J., Antonio, and Papá stayed by them playing games. When I ducked my head out of the kitchen to mention that the stray beagle needed to go out (which I had sensed), Eduardo took him down to the street.

Mamá and Abuelita joined me in the kitchen. Mamá hugged me as soon as she came in. "So, you've been there!"

Abuelita gave a knowing nod. They set to work with me on the cleanup chores.

Mamá said, "Well, don't just stand there—tell us everything."

It all bubbled up inside me, and I started to talk and talk and talk. With each part of the adventure that I told, I relived the wonder, the uncertainty, the sense of responsibility, the discouragements, and the triumphs of my quest. Abuelita made *chocolatl* while we finished the dishes and the kitchen cleanup.

Then, together, we drank the steaming liquid that was so important to our family line, and I finished my story.

Mamá and Abuelita were amazed when I told them about the jaguar and later about the spider. They were also extremely interested in my mapmaking. When I finished my story, Mamá said, "*Mi'ja,* you did something very special in Aventurine."

"*El corazon es su mapa,*" Abuelita reminded me.

"You were right," I admitted. "I didn't believe it

at first when you told me, but I did have to follow my heart to make the map."

"And by following your heart, you gave a very special gift to Aventurine," Mamá said. "No other fairy-godmother-in-training has ever attempted to make a map. And you did it, purely for the love of it."

"Does that mean I'm done with the fun parts, now that I've gone on a quest and made the map? I know that my job is to help innocents in this world, but I still want lots of adventures!"

Mamá chuckled. "No matter what your calling is, as a fairy godmother, I can promise that your life will involve many, many more adventures."

Abuelita took a sip of her *chocolatl* and sighed. "And while you are waiting for those adventures, your mother and I can tell you about what we did when we were in Aventurine."

The next day was Monday, a day hated around the world by kids and parents both. All in all, there is not a day of the week that gets more complaints than Monday—except maybe Friday the thirteenth, but that's for a totally different reason. I was actually looking forward to Monday, and Monday didn't disappoint me.

When my alarm went off, I bounced out of bed,

even though it was still pitch-black outside. After a quick shower, I put on my school uniform, put my books and schoolwork into my backpack, and headed down to the bakery. Without waiting for someone to tell me what to do and then grumbling about it, I turned on the lights, preheated the ovens, and was just starting to brew a pot of coffee when my parents came in with Abuelita.

Papá blinked at me a couple of times, as if confused by what he was seeing, and said, "Thank you, *mi'ja.* Would you please—"

"Start the first batch of bread?" I asked, surprising him again. I knew the drill, though I usually resisted doing things until I was told to. "I'm on it!"

I dashed into the back and started measuring ingredients into the massive Hobart mixer that kneaded the bread dough. I heard an explosion of comments in Spanish, then laughter from the front of the shop, where my parents and Abuelita were pouring themselves coffee.

The early morning seemed to flash by like a lightning bolt. My brothers came in, and I teased them about being sleepyheads. When the customers arrived, I chatted with them and rang up their purchases while my parents expertly packed up their orders to go. Abuelita served coffee, tea, and hot chocolate. The aroma of chocolate in the air energized me further. Was there any smell more wonderful?

Before I knew it, it was time for school. Now, you might think that after spending time in Aventurine, being back in the normal world at a normal school with normal people might seem dull and boring. It wasn't. The subjects in every class seemed more important now. I noticed things I never had before, like how shy my best friend, Malia, was when talking in class, or the way my algebra teacher, Mrs. Dixon, looked for ways to encourage every student in the class and make equations less intimidating, or that Ms. Alessandro (who cooks in our cafeteria) played flute after school in the music room while our music teacher, Mr. Bumatay, accompanied her on piano.

The colors outside the windows seemed brighter and richer. I looked at everyone differently now, wondering if there might be magic in someone else I knew. Queen Patchouli had said that if I met another potential fairy-godmother-in-training, I would be able to sense it if I was paying attention.

After school, Cody, Malia, and I went for a walk through Central Park. That's where the coolest thing happened. From everywhere, all around the park, I felt subtle waves of mood and feeling—a squirrel frantically storing away food for winter, a golden retriever thrilled to be out in the fresh air for a romp with her master.

Then I caught a sense of edginess and irritability. Looking around, I noticed that it came from a horse stopped beside a tree not far from us. The rider was a little younger than me and was dressed in jodhpurs and tall boots. She dismounted and stood beside the horse, whispering soothing words, but the horse was having none of it.

"I'll be right back," I said to Cody and Malia. I went over to where the perplexed girl was trying to gentle her mount. The horse's ears drew back and twitched. The bay mare looked nothing like Kir, but I was reminded of him nonetheless.

"Is it okay if I touch her?" I asked the girl, reaching out to pat the horse. She nodded.

I spoke comforting words in a whisper to the mare. I was completely aware that I wasn't in a magical land anymore, but I thought, *Why not give it a shot?* So I sent out soothing questions: *What's wrong, girl? Is something bothering you?*

I didn't actually expect it to work, but . . . *there*! All of a sudden, there it was.

"She's not usually like this," the girl said. "I guess

I'll have to take her back to the stables now."

"Wait," I said. "There's a bur under her saddle blanket, over here on the left side, under the girth." I slid my fingers under as far as I could reach and felt something small, hard, and prickly, which I managed to work loose and pull out. The horse whickered and stomped her hoof. I reached in again and felt around to make sure I had gotten everything. The horse assured me that I had.

"I think she'll be fine now," I said.

The girl thanked me, shaking her head in amazement. She swung back onto the saddle and rode away.

Well, that answered that question! It might be different, but the magic—the gift I'd been given to sense the needs of the innocent and to help them—that worked, even in the middle of New York City. And Queen Patchouli had also assured me that my dreams would bring me back to Aventurine. I was grinning as I walked back to join Malia and Cody. It was going to be a great year, in my dreams and out of them.

Acknowledgments

My best friend is an archaeologist with a specialty in the Maya. She let me read all of her research and reference books so that I could have intelligent conversations with her while she wrote her wonderful book and the script for her film on the history of chocolate. I imagined the smell of chocolate as we drove and talked for seven hours back and forth from Austin to Marfa. Thank you, M, for all you have done to support my creativity over the course of my career. I also want to thank my Cuban family, who are now spread about the country from Minnesota to Houston. My memory of Latin music and dancing in our living room on Saturday nights has shaped me. There is nothing lovelier than a big family dancing and eating together—while debating world affairs, of course. Poochie, Lita, Louie, Dora, Lydia, Matilda, Uncle Tony Baloney, Louis, and Martha will live on in my Latina dreams and *mi vida dorada*!

About the Author

Jan Bozarth was raised in an international family in Texas in the sixties, the daughter of a Cuban mother and a Welsh father. She danced in a ballet company at eleven, started a dream journal at thirteen, joined a surf club at sixteen, studied flower essences at eighteen, and went on to study music, art, and poetry in college. As a girl, she dreamed of a life that would weave these different interests together. Her dream came true when she grew up and had a big family and a music and writing career. Jan is now a grandmother and writes stories and songs for young people. She often works with her own grown-up children, who are musicians and artists in Austin, Texas. (Sometimes Jan is even the fairy godmother who encourages them to believe in their dreams!) Jan credits her own mother, Dora, with handing down her wisdom: Dream big and never give up.

Lilu's Book

Coming soon!

Turn the page to meet Lilu!
She's about to go on her first adventure to Aventurine—*without* her identical twin!

(Dear Reader, please note that the following excerpt may change for the actual printing of *Lilu's Book*.)

From *Lilu's Book*

The back porch had always been my home away from home. At the other end was a futon with an oversized cushion covered in fat blue and white stripes. I'd slept on it a number of times, and I always woke up feeling fresher, more alive.

Three sides of the porch were screened, and the one wall was lined with old-fashioned shelves. Each shelf held baskets and jars filled with seashells. Our seashell collections were also strung together and hung around the room.

"You were terrific today at the pool," said Mom.

I shrugged. Sitting so close to her, feeling the warmth of her skin, I felt cozy and safe.

"The best part, I think, was seeing you in the stands next to Dad."

Oh no! That just slipped out! I'm such a dope.

This is exactly the type of thing moms are looking for when they set us up for special bonding time.

She turned toward me and the swing creaked. "You miss him a lot, don't you?"

I dropped my head back and let out a long sigh. "Mom," I groaned. "I know you guys aren't getting back together. And I know it's not my fault or 'our fault,' like some kids think. And I know you're very happy, okay?"

"Well, sounds like you've got it all figured out. Eat your pie, sweetheart," Mom said.

I took a large forkful of the creamy sweet potato pie. "Mom, this is delicious. You know I could eat sweet potato pie every day!"

Mom set her plate on her lap and turned toward me. Her eyes studied me for a second, and then she said, "How about you and Tandy? Everything okay?"

Moms have that way about them, you know. They're more than smart—they're clever. Here she was letting me talk about her and Dad and everything, then out of nowhere she hits me with what's really bugging me. I guess thinking I could hide it from her was silly. Mom always figures things out.

Still, if I had any chance of avoiding more mother-daughter bonding, I had to rely on the one trick in every kid's book: denial.

"Mom, me and Tan are fine. I'm fine. Really."

"So you're telling me you're excited about moving and delighted with all the changes and ecstatic that your sister is developing other interests and is not spending as much time with you?" she asked.

I studied the pie on my plate and pushed a piece of crust back and forth.

"I . . ." My voice broke. I tried to say something lighthearted, but it just got caught in my throat.

She reached over and squeezed my knee. "Lilu, baby, having you girls has been a constant blessing, a gift. I've watched you blossom, watched your friendship, your special connection. I've watched it and loved it. But I know the two of you are at an age where you might not be quite as identical as you once were. Tandy is getting really involved in her acting. She's great at it. But I see the way you get whenever that stuff comes up. I guess what I want to say to you is don't be afraid to let her go. Once you let her go, you give yourself permission to be all of what *Lilu* was meant to be. Permission to accept all the blessings the good Lord has in store just for you. You are a rare and beautiful creature, Lilu Hart. Don't be afraid of your uniqueness."

Nothing to do with a speech like that but eat a few forkfuls of pie and let it sink in. Mom hummed while she ate, as though she was humming the same tune that the ocean was playing with its waves. The tall, lush sweet grass and foxtail alongside the house swished and swayed in the wind, lending a backup chorus.

"This is for you," she said. Mom's softly spoken words coasted on ocean breezes. She held out her hand and the gauzy moonlight flitted over the object in her outstretched palm.

It was a shell unlike any I'd ever seen. I reached out and took it from her.

"It's shaped like a crescent moon," I said.

Mom nodded, her half smile now almost hidden behind her forkful of pie.

"Hey, Mom, have you packed all the old seashell books? I'd love to look this one up. It's amazing!"

She sat her plate on the floor, lifted her iced tea, and took a long swallow. Then she said, "It *is* amazing, Lilu. But you won't find it in any book. It is one of a kind, made by the sea and the moon specifically for our people, our ancestors, and passed down from generation to generation."

"Like the baskets?" I squeezed my hand shut, pressing the cool, unusual shell into my skin. Then my hand opened wide as my mind whirred in fear of damaging something so precious.

"Sort of like the baskets. But the crescent moon came before the baskets. Without the pure magic of this moon's light, our family might never have found its way, would never have understood its purpose."

I frowned. "You're talking about Aventurine again, aren't you?"

"Let's take a walk," she said.

The screen door snapped shut like a turtle's mouth. As we moved toward the ocean, I glanced over my shoulder. Our house was candy pink with big, rolled tiles on the roof called barrel tiles. Black shutters sat beside the windows. On nights like tonight, after a huge afternoon storm, we opened the windows to allow the ocean air inside.

An occasional strong gust blew from the ocean, making me glad that I had used a red scarf as a headband to keep my unruly curls out of my face. Tall sea grasses and reeds bent and swayed, at times whipping about with such force, they looked like the mane of a charging lion.

Mom led me to a jagged rock formation and began to climb. We were careful to place our feet in the crags and craters, moving carefully until we reached a lip of the rock face that flattened. With my eyes closed, I filled my lungs with the beautiful ocean scent, fresh and briny and alive. Whenever I was this close to the ocean, especially at night, it became a symphony in my head.

Mom interrupted my thoughts. "Lilu, you know your aunt Mary and I have talked a lot about Aventurine with you girls over the years."

I nodded.

"Well, now it's your time," she said. "I didn't know which of you girls would be first, but now I know it's you."

"Mom, you've always talked about Aventurine; you talk about it being such a cool, magical place. A place for strong women to figure out who they are and become fairy godmothers . . ."

"That's right."

"So . . . it's real? I thought it was just some sort of bedtime story."

Mom's laughter was deep and sweet. "No, baby, that was no bedtime story. Aventurine is definitely real."

My knees buckled. My hand shut tight, and the shell dug painfully into my palm. The sea bubbled into froth.

"Whoa!" Mom reached out and grabbed me. She helped me sit on the flat part of the craggy rock and didn't take her arms from around me until I was sitting, facing the ocean, feeling the dampness of the surf against my skin.

"Umm, maybe next time you share life-changing news with me, we can do it someplace more stable? Remember, I'm the one who isn't that good with change!"

"Don't worry, Lilu. You'll be fine." Mom squeezed my shoulder and I let myself lean into her, just like on the porch. Then she lightly tapped the fist where I was squeezing the shell.

"Relax," she said. "You won't lose it. When you need it, it will find you. Aventurine will teach you how to use it."

I frowned. This was crazy! Mom knew I was the practical one. The kid who always had to have proof. Tandy was the one who still pretended to be a mermaid and chased dragons.

Mom smiled. "I know you sometimes want more facts before you make a plan, but now I'm going to ask for a favor."

"What is it?"

When she looked at me, she took my hands into hers and said, "I want you to stop thinking so hard about how everything should be and what pieces should go where."

Now it was my turn to smile. She had me. I sighed. "Okay, Mom. So, tell me *again* about Aventurine. Remind me how this is supposed to work."

"Early on, I knew I was blessed with the gift of weaving stories," she said.

"I thought our family's skill is weaving *baskets*. I find seashells, keep our inventory, and plan how to sell the stuff Tan and I make. But she's the one who can actually *make* things. The weaving and crocheting and all the crafts, that's what you and Tandy do. I don't have that gift."

"Those are skills passed down from generation to generation. Skills that, if you believe in yourself and have faith, you, too, can develop. Or maybe develop other skills that work just as well. But my true 'gift,' that thing I knew I was meant to do more than anything else, that was writing. It was what I'd dreamed of since I was a little girl. Writing allows me to speak with people in their language. Not the language of their ears, but the language of their hearts.

"Our family comes from the Songa Lineage. Crafting a story isn't so different from crafting a basket. Instead of sturdy reeds, I take words out of the air and shape them into thoughts and emotions, information and delight."

I nodded. I hadn't thought of it that way.

"So," I said, "what is the Songo heritage thing about?"

"The Songa Lineage. When famine threatened our ancestors' survival in Africa, our queen spoke to the moon."

My mouth dropped open. I said, "And the moon spoke back?"

Mom smiled, her teeth as white as the shell. "More like the moon goddesses. It turns out the moon needed us, too. It had gone off track and pulled the tides out of alignment. Our great ancestor, a woman known as Mama Akuko, herself a fairy godmother, saved the moon and the tides."

When I just stared at her, Mom said, "In some African languages, *Akuko* means 'youngest twin.'"

Now my jaw dropped.

"We have ancestors who were twins?"

"Of course," Mom said. "You know twin genes run in certain families. If you're a twin, there's a good chance you have ancestors who were twins."

"And this woman, Mama Akusa . . ."

"Mama Akuko," she corrected.

"Yes, Mama Akuko. What did she do for the moon?"

"Mama Akuko was an expert weaver. So expert that she found a way to tug the moonbeams and guide the tides back on course."

"But how?" I asked.

"Well, my love, that is a secret that stays with Mama Akuko and the moon goddesses, a secret you must earn," she said.

Something in her stance was so . . . *real.* The angle of her body, the tilt of her head, the way her shoulders pulled back.

"How . . . how will I do that? Earn the secret, I mean. And what if I can't do what it takes? What if I get to Aventurine and cannot do what they need me to do?" My voice faltered on that last part.

Then, before Mom could answer my questions, I hit her with another:

"Why me and not Tandy?"

"This is about you, the youngest twin. Mama Akuko represents all those twins who came to be even though they were unexpected and unprepared for. I've told you girls the story over and over about how shocked your father and I were when you arrived."

"I know, I know. For some reason I didn't show up on the ultrasound. What can I say? I've always been camera-shy."

We both laughed. Then Mom said, "Aventurine

is the perfect place to figure out what distinguishes you in the world—not just from your sister, but from everyone else. There is nothing to fear in Aventurine. You go there in your dreams."

Suddenly questions rushed at me, but Mom held up a finger. "Shhh," she said. "I know you have questions, and I know you have much to learn. Keep the shell with you tonight; keep it near you while you sleep. Don't worry about finding Aventurine. Aventurine will find you!"

Have you read the first
Fairy Godmother Academy book?

Birdie's Book

Available now!

Will Kerka learn the right Kalis moves in time to save her sisters?
Find out in

Available now!

Can't get enough of the Fairy Godmother Academy?

Check out the website for music, games, and more!
FairyGodmotherAcademy.com

The Fairy Godmother Academy is on Facebook!
Become a fan and get all of the latest news and updates.

Download your Wisdom Card today.

www.randomhouse.com/teens/fga

Exclusive, collectible Wisdom Cards are key to the story for each book's heroine!

Wisdom Cards are the rewards of the Fairy Godmother Academy, and you earn them by completing the missions. Some are easy; some are difficult. Some can only be tackled by a group, while others must be faced by you alone. Join the missions in any order you like to earn Wisdom Cards and add jewels to your crown.

Join the Fairy Godmother Academy!

Visit FairyGodmotherAcademy.com

700